MW01286353

COUNTER TERROR
A Jake Adams International Espionage Thriller #13

by
Trevor Scott

United States of America

Also by Trevor Scott

Max Kane Series
Truth or Justice
Stolen Honor
Relative Impact

Karl Adams Series
The Man from Murmansk
Siberian Protocol

Jake Adams International Espionage Thriller Series
Fatal Network (#1)
Extreme Faction (#2)
The Dolomite Solution (#3)
Vital Force (#4)
Rise of the Order (#5)
The Cold Edge (#6)
Without Options (#7)
The Stone of Archimedes (#8)
Lethal Force (#9)
Rising Tiger (#10)
Counter Caliphate (#11)
Gates of Dawn (#12)
Counter Terror (#13)

Covert Network (#14)
Shadow Warrior (#15)
Sedition (#16)

<u>The Tony Caruso Mystery Series</u>
Boom Town (#1)
Burst of Sound (#2)
Running Game (#3)

<u>The Chad Hunter Espionage Thriller Series</u>
Hypershot (#1)
Global Shot (#2)
Cyber Shot (#3)

<u>The Keenan Fitzpatrick Mystery Series</u>
Isolated (#1)
Burning Down the House (#2)
Witness to Murder (#3)

<u>Other Mysteries and Thrillers</u>
Cantina Valley
Edge of Delirium
Strong Conviction
Fractured State (A Novella)
The Nature of Man

Discernment
Way of the Sword
Drifting Back
The Dawn of Midnight
The Hobgoblin of the Redwoods
Duluthians: A Collection of Short Stories

This is a work of fiction. All characters and events portrayed in this novel are fictitious and not intended to represent real people or places. All rights reserved. No part of this book may be reproduced in any manner whatsoever without written permission of the author.

Counter Terror
Copyright © 2016 by Trevor Scott
United States of America
trevorscott.com

Cover image of shooter by Deanna Quinto Larson
Background cover image by author

For Trevor Schmidt
An outstanding young science fiction author

1

Rome, Italy

Rain drifted across the *Piazza del Papolo*, obscuring the People's Square that was lit by dozens of ornate lights. The chill November breeze brought with it an ethereal set of clouds resembling apparitions flying in formation, like a massive flock of ghostly snow geese.

Jake Adams lifted the collar on his leather jacket to ward off the bite from the cold moisture, and then cast his gaze upon the sparse crowd moving through the piazza with quick paces. This was not an evening for lingering, he thought. Perhaps that would be his best indication of his contact, who was at least ten minutes late now. The man would be moving slowly like a tortoise among a group of hares.

Something big was heading toward Rome, Jake knew, and he was determined to discover what form that would take. Most of the major cities of Europe had seen terrorist attacks over the years, but Rome had somehow escaped that destiny. Jake guessed the terrorists were suicidal and crazy, but they also knew that attacking the seat of the Roman Catholic religion would be like dropping bombs in the shape of pigs on Mecca and Medina.

Jake held tight against the western wall, which gave him a perfect view of the wide piazza, while allowing him a quick escape around the wall toward his car parked just a block away near the Tiber River.

He had been commissioned to meet with a man with contacts throughout the various nefarious organizations across Italy—from anarchists to religious zealots. Jake's contacts had confirmed that Sergio Russo was a capo in the Calabrese Malavita. The only photo Jake had of the guy was a few years old and wasn't very detailed. But the man's dossier described one distinguishing feature that could not be denied—a birthmark at the right temple in the shape of the Island of Malta, running from the hairline to his right eye.

There he was, Jake thought. Moving in from the south side of the piazza was a slight man in jeans and a dark green rain jacket, the hood pulled over his head.

"Got him," Jake said into his comm unit.

"Roger that," Alexandra said. This was his girlfriend's first foray into the field since giving birth to their daughter nearly six months ago. Alexandra was positioned at the north side of the piazza near the entrance to a Leonardo da Vinci museum, which was closed at this hour.

Jake's contact moved to the center obelisk statue that towered above the piazza, where he stopped and swiveled his head. Then he lit a cigarette, the all clear sign.

Instead of concentrating solely on Russo, Jake kept an eye on the perimeter as he walked out to the center of the piazza.

When Jake got to the base of the obelisk, he glanced up at the man to size him up. He fit the description. Jake climbed the few stairs to the base of the tall obelisk and stood within a few feet of his contact.

His contact said in Italian, "Why do they call this a square?"

"I know," Jake said, also in Italian. "It's obviously a circle."

Their code phrase complete, Jake moved in closer and finally got a good look at the Mafia captain. Russo was somewhere in his mid-fifties, with speckled silver hair receding at the temples, allowing Jake to see the

Malta birthmark. He had a three-day growth of beard just like Jake, although the Mafia man had more gray.

"Do you speak English?" Jake asked.

"Some. Your Italian is littered with Calabrese."

"The true Italian," Jake said, trying his best to compliment the man. He knew that those from Calabria, the southernmost province of Italy, were staunchly affiliated to the region. It was like the Texas of Italy.

Russo smiled and showed Jake a set of imperfect teeth with crooked canines, stained yellow from his smoking habit. He worked on his cigarette, putting the tip to a bright orange and squinting as he let out a breath of smoke.

"Do you know the irony of this place?" Russo asked.

Jake shrugged.

"For centuries they used to execute citizens here," Russo said.

"Why the Egyptian obelisk?" Jake asked.

Russo shrugged. "Augustus had it brought here from Egypt in ten B.C. It was first erected in the Circus Maximus."

In Jake's earpiece, Alexandra said, "Tell him to get on with it."

"Enough history lessons," Jake said. "I was told you have some information for me."

The Italian switched back to his native tongue and said, "You know that we work on a code of silence."

Jake knew. "But."

"But this could be very important to the survival of the western world, especially Italy."

Jake swiveled his eyes to scan the area behind the Mafia man and to his blind spot. He would have to rely on Alexandra to cover that which he couldn't see. And also he had to depend somewhat on the Italian to sense something out of the ordinary.

"And?" Jake asked.

"My people are concerned."

Jake guessed that the Calabrese Malavita didn't rattle easily. "What do you know?"

"Roma will be a target soon," Russo said.

"I could hear that on the evening news."

Russo lit a second cigarette from the butt of his first one and nodded his head. Then he flicked the old butt into a fountain with a lion spitting water. "This is true. But it's one thing to speculate, and another to know certain facts."

"We need specifics," Alexandra said in Jake's ear.

"When and where?" Jake asked.

Russo's eyes shifted and then narrowed with uncertainty. "I don't know that for sure."

"Rome is a big city with many potential targets."

"I know. And they have increased security at most ancient cites. But it's still not enough."

Jake had observed that himself recently. Although they had a few heavily-armed units in place at high impact targets, it wouldn't take that much to mitigate their efforts. As he pondered that, his eyes caught a man approaching from the south end who looked out of ordinary. It wasn't his clothes, but it was more his demeanor as he approached that made the hairs on the back of Jake's neck stand up. Now he shifted his gaze toward the east side of the piazza and noticed another man who was walking with purpose toward the center obelisk. That was the problem. The man wasn't making a normal path through the piazza. He was moving toward them.

"Jake, you've got company," Alexandra said in his ear.

"I know," Jake said. "One at my twelve and one at my three."

Russo looked confused. "What?"

Jake instinctively unzipped his jacket allowing for easy access to his 9mm Glock under his left arm. "Did you bring some friends?"

The Mafia man shifted his eyes. "No. I came alone." Then he seemed to understand that all was not right with this meeting.

"A third man behind you," Alexandra said, her voice professional and clear. "Seventy-five meters out."

"Coming your way," Jake said, and then grasped the Italian man by his arm and started to round the obelisk and down the stone steps on the other side. Then to Russo Jake said, "Are you armed?"

"Of course," Russo said.

Jake drew his Glock and held it against his right leg.

"I've got the car," Alexandra said.

The problem, of course, was that there was a lot of open space across this massive piazza before they reached safety. It was the reason for meeting here in the first place, but it left them vulnerable during a retreat.

Suddenly, the relative quiet was broken by the sound of gunshots. Jake swiveled around and shot twice at the shooter. Then the two of them took off running toward the north entrance to the square.

More gunshots.

The Mafia man now had his gun out and started shooting like a madman, nearly emptying his magazine on the three men on their tail. But his shots were erratic and hit nothing.

By the time they got to the north end, Jake could see the dark brown Fiat Tipo he had acquired earlier that evening.

Alexandra was behind the wheel and skidded to a stop just long enough for Jake to get in the front passenger seat and Russo to pile in the back seat. As they pulled away, the tires spinning on the wet cobblestone streets, bullets flew at them striking the side and back of the car.

The Mafia capo was hunkered down in the back seat swearing in Italian.

Jake turned to see the men climb into a black Audi. Damn, Jake thought. No way could they outrun that car.

Now Russo leaned forward and said, "Who is this fine lady?"

Alexandra shook her head.

"My associate," Jake said, not wanting to give away any more information than he needed to at this time. "Who followed you to this meeting?"

"How do you know they didn't follow you?" Russo asked.

Alexandra huffed out a breath of air.

Jake said, "Who knew you were meeting here tonight?"

"Just my boss. Nobody else."

"Does he trust you?" Jake asked.

"He was the one who told me to meet with you. He has a mutual friend of yours."

That would be Jake's Spanish billionaire benefactor, Carlos Gomez. The man who had sent Jake here as well. Did he have a leak in his organization? Anything was possible.

Alexandra ran through the gears like a formula one driver, turning around corners like she was on the Circuit de Monaco. By now they were a block from the Tiber River.

Jake glanced back and saw that the Audi was slowly moving in on them. "We can't beat that car," he said.

"We'll see," Alexandra said, downshifting and rounding a corner. Then she hit the gas and ran through the gears again.

"Don't cross the river," Russo said. "Turn left."

Without thinking, Alexandra did as he said. Now they were on a wider street and she could pick up the pace. The only cross streets were for bridges, and many of those were pedestrian only. But this also made it easier for the Audi to catch them, since they were much faster.

The light ahead changed to red, but Alexandra didn't even tap the brakes. She flew through the intersection, narrowly missing a car that had to stop for her. Horns blared at them.

A block later and they hit a bump in the road that made them sail into the air. They hit with a hard bang, the crappy, stiff suspension bottoming out. Jake turned and saw the Audi barely getting any air.

"What the hell is going on?" Jake asked Russo.

The Mafia captain simply shrugged, and Jake could tell the man was equally baffled.

"Boys, we've got another problem," Alexandra said.

Jake looked back and saw two Polizia cars, lights flashing, in hot pursuit. He whirred his window down and finally heard the sirens.

By now they were across the river from Castel St. Angelo. In seconds they would be near the Vatican.

"Turn left," Jake said.

"No," Russo said.

But Alexandra had already made the turn.

"This will bring us right to the heart of downtown and the *Colosseo*."

Jake knew this. But instead of staying on the main street, he directed Alexandra to turn right through residential neighborhoods. By going this way, the Polizia would have a nearly impossible time trying to set up a road block.

Bullets continued to come from the Audi, but they were also forced to shoot behind them at the Polizia cars. Occasionally, Jake and Russo would return fire.

"Jake. We've got a problem," Alexandra said.

Looking ahead, Jake could see a busy street with a steady stream of cars.

"Cut through," Jake said.

She turned her head for just a second and then nodded. Without slowing, she timed the traffic ahead as best as she could. But she clipped the back end of one car, which made that car careen into another, leading to a complete pileup. By now, though, they had exited the other side with only minor damage to the front end.

Jake turned and saw the snarl of cars at the massive intersection. "We're free. Head to the autostrada."

Alexandra let out a relieving breath and loosened her grip on the steering wheel.

Russo leaned forward and said, "How do they say this in English? I have partial wood?"

"Something like that," Jake said. "But she's taken."

Amalfi, Italy

A distinguished man of some five or six decades stood against the rail on the promenade above the break wall for the sea. He wore a fine suit with an overcoat to fight off the night chill, and he stroked his long, silver goatee. He had just eaten a fine meal of pasta and sea creatures, from fish to octopus. He followed that with a shot of Sambuca. Then he went for his stroll, only to be disturbed in an extreme emergency. His men knew what that meant.

So, when his most trusted advisor approached through his security detail, it could only mean one thing—something had gone wrong in Rome.

"Speak to me," the boss said.

His man stammered slightly, a nervous tick and no fault of his own. The man had been beaten relentlessly as a child until he finally couldn't take it any longer and ran away from home, living on the streets of Naples until he could work his way into the underworld of drug trafficking and other nefarious criminal activity.

"Calm down, Poco. Just tell me."

The younger man took in a deep breath and finally said, "We followed the Malavita Capo as ordered. He met with another man in *Piazza del Papolo*." He hesitated. Perhaps that was a mistake. "Shots were exchanged."

"I told you just to observe for now," the boss said.

"Yes, sir. But this other man moved like a *grande gatto. La tigre.*"

The distinguished man stroked his beard in contemplation. He had heard that the Spaniard was bringing in a professional. And that was why he had sent his men. Just to assess the situation. "What happened."

After more hesitation and stammering, the younger man finally said, "A car chase. The Polizia got involved."

That wasn't a problem. He could deal with the Polizia. "And?"

"They got away. Russo and this new man. And a third person. A very good driver."

Not a total failure, the boss guessed. He had hoped to fly under the radar for now. But this could just mean he needed to move up his timeline. He glanced up to the sky and gazed at the swirling clouds which periodically exposed the stars. Then he tried to run the math through his head, but it wasn't coming to him. Not entirely. He would need one of his whiteboards to make sense of all of this.

"All right," the boss finally said. "Put the word out on the street to find this capo Russo. But don't kill him. Not yet. The last thing we need is a war with the Calabrese Malavita."

"Yes, sir."

His young man went away, and he again considered the equations in his mind. But the numbers weren't adding up. He would need to get back to his lab in Calabria.

2

Tropea, Italy

Jake and Alexandra had traveled through the night from Rome to Calabria, getting to their home overlooking the Tyrrhenian Sea around three in the morning. First, they had dropped off Sergio Russo at a train station on the outskirts of Rome. Then they had dumped the damaged Fiat and picked up Alexandra's Alfa Romeo where they had left it near the Fiumicino Airport. Jake took over the driving, making it to Calabria in record time.

Four hours later, Jake had heard the first whining from his daughter. But their babysitter was still on the job. He rolled over in bed and kissed Alexandra on the nape of her neck.

"Go back to sleep," she mumbled.

"I don't want that."

"You always want that."

She rolled over and her right breast almost slapped him across the face.

"It doesn't help that you sleep in the nude," he said.

"I could switch to flannel."

"Let's not go crazy, Alexandra." His eyes settled on her bare breasts.

"You're telling me you don't want to make sex?"

"I mean, I would take one for the team. But that's not why I'm awake."

"I feel something hard."

"Sorry, that's my gun."

"I know what you call it."

"No, I mean, this is my actual gun. My Glock." He retrieved his gun and showed her. "Sorry. It must have slipped from under the pillow."

"Sure." Alexandra frowned. "All right. Now you've got me all worked up. Take me hard and fast and let me shower." She reached down and found his willing erection. "I knew it." Without saying another word, she climbed up and took him all at once, riding him like he was a bronco. When she was done, she dismounted perfectly and walked to the en suite bathroom. With a heavy workout of running and martial arts training, she had already lost all of the weight from giving birth six months ago.

"I'll make you a cappuccino," he said.

She waved her hand at him as she stepped into the shower. He felt so cheap. Satisfied, but cheap.

He got dressed and wandered out into the kitchen. Their babysitter held their daughter, Emma, feeding her a bottle of formula in a rocker in the adjoining living room.

Jake waved at Monica, who smiled and nodded back. While he made a cappuccino, he considered their good fortune having Monica watch their baby. She was Alexandra's second cousin and a retired German Polizei officer. Monica had raised three girls of her own, but they were all out of the house with families of their own. When Alexandra asked her if she wanted to come to sunny Italy for a while to help with Emma, it didn't take much convincing. She had divorced her husband a decade ago, and finally felt useful again. Some would see her short gray hair and stocky build and immediately think lesbian. But that wasn't the case. Monica had kept her hair that way since her first year as a Polizei officer, when some dirtbag grabbed her long hair and swung her around like a ragdoll. She would never let that happen again.

Steaming the milk, Jake completed his cappuccino and started a second one for Alexandra. He knew she would be in the shower for a while, though.

"You got in late," Monica said, her English quite good and getting better. They had decided to teach Emma English, German and Italian simultaneously.

He finished Alexandra's cappuccino and let it sit on the counter. "Sorry about that. Did we wake you?" Jake rounded the island and stooped down for a better look at his little angel.

"I had my Walther out before you came through the front gate," she said. "You have better security than our military in Germany."

"That's where I learned my trade," he said, and then drank most of his cappuccino.

"How was Rome?"

"Boring. You've seen one two-thousand-year-old building, why look at another?"

Alexandra came out of the bedroom and found her cappuccino. She took a sip and then glanced at Jake. "What? No special leaf or clover or something cool?"

Jake shrugged. "I get less creative with four or five hours of sleep."

"You could have slept in," Monica said. "I'm fine with Emma. She's a sweetheart."

Alexandra came in and kneeled down, kissing her daughter on the forehead. "Yes, she is." Then she glanced at her cousin. "Did he tell you he almost got us killed last night?"

Monica looked concerned. "No."

"She's exaggerating," Jake said.

"I am not. Three men. Four with the driver. Tried to blow our heads off."

"I was more concerned about your driving," Jake said. "Have her tell you about smashing the car through an intersection."

"Not the Alfa," Monica said.

Alexandra shook her head. "No. It was a borrowed car. And it was barely scratched."

Jake heard his phone buzz, so he finished off his cappuccino and found his phone. Very few people had his number. Other than those in this room, that included just his son Karl, his old CIA friend Kurt Jenkins, and the billionaire Carlos Gomez. He checked the text and saw that it was the latter.

Glancing back at Alexandra, Jake said, "Carlos heard about our Roman adventure."

"Is he still in the Tropea harbor?" Alexandra asked.

Carlos Gomez spent about ninety percent of his time cruising around the Mediterranean in his massive yacht. Some thought he was afraid to fly, but Jake knew that wasn't the case. The man just loved the sea. And tax shelters.

"I'm guessing so," Jake said, texting back to his friend and benefactor. A few years ago, Jake had taken a job with the billionaire to secure the release of his nephew and a number of other medical relief workers taken hostage by a radical Muslim terrorist group in Morocco. Since then Jake had done a few more missions. One in the Baltics had gotten him shot in the gut for his efforts. But the man paid well and seemed to be concerned with righteous causes. So, the risk was worth the benefits. His daughter Emma would have anything she wanted from life.

A second later and he got a text from Carlos.

"He's still here," Jake said. "Wants us to do lunch on his yacht at noon."

"Sounds lovely," Alexandra said. "Have fun."

"He specifically said he'd like to meet you. Something about meeting the crazy German who drives like a maniac."

"He did not." She grabbed for Jake's phone.

Jake shrugged. "It was implied." He smiled and added, "Any way I can get you to clean my gun from last night while I take a run?"

"I'll do that," Monica chimed in. "So Alexandra can spend some time with Emma."

They all agreed nonverbally. Jake wasn't a huge runner, but since his last bullet injury he felt the need to get in better shape. He was normally inclined to spend most of his exercise time in the weight room or perfecting his martial arts, beating the crap out of various bags. He had also helped Alexandra get back into fighting shape following her pregnancy. She was always a great fighter, but in the past six months her training seemed to take on a new vigor.

Once Jake ran over 5K down the shore, and then worked out in the gym, he showered and was ready for his meeting with Carlos Gomez. Despite having worked for the man for a number of years, Carlos had never met Alexandra. Of course, usually their meetings had been in far off locations, and Alexandra had been preoccupied with her pregnancy.

The two of them drove their old Fiat into Tropea, parking in a downtown open lot that was seemingly controlled by a fat Italian with food stains on his strained sports T-shirt. This was a free city parking lot, but there was always some low-life douche bag who wanted to make a buck off of tourists in Calabria. Although they were now considered locals, Jake guessed the guy saw Alexandra and guessed German tourist. She told the guy to fuck off in perfect Italian, but he was still reluctant to go away.

Jake moved in close and whispered something into the fat man's ear. The guy raised his brows and slowly backed away to a plastic chair he had set up under a tree.

Jake and Alexandra walked down the cobblestone street toward a restaurant overlooking the beaches down the high cliff.

"What did you say to the fat man?" Alexandra asked.

"I simply said we were here to do lunch with Sergio Russo."

"Wow," Alexandra said. "That man must have some pull around here. Then why did we have to meet him in Rome?"

"Russo is the capo for all of Vibo. And I don't know why we had to meet in Rome. You can ask him at lunch."

"He'll be here?"

"Apparently."

They got to the restaurant and pizzeria on the precipice of the cliff exactly at noon. Initially, they were stopped at the door until the Spaniard's men recognized Jake. Then they tried on a smile and let them pass. Carlos Gomez sat at the best seat in the restaurant. To his left was the Malavita Captain, Sergio Russo. Both men respectfully rose to greet Alexandra with a kiss on both cheeks. Russo couldn't keep his eyes off of her substantial breasts, which had not been in display the night before in Rome.

All four of them took their seats.

Jake said, "It looks like we have the place to ourselves."

Carlos smiled. He was an unassuming billionaire with a distinguished look, but who wore unpretentious clothing, blending in to nearly any setting. Today the man simply wore blue jeans and a black sweater. The only indicator of opulence was his expensive deck shoes and his Swiss watch. "This is one of my properties. We will not be disturbed. My chef will cook you anything, but I must say that there is fresh tuna from this morning."

Jake and Alexandra agreed to that. One could only eat so much pizza.

They had Peroni beers all around while they waited for their meals.

Carlos got right into it. "Rome was almost a disaster. But the two of you saved the day."

Jake looked at Russo and said, "Did you come up with how those people found us?"

"There are always those below us who would like our job," Russo said casually. Somehow the man's English had improved overnight.

"So, one of your men sold you out," Jake surmised.

Russo glanced at Carlos Gomez for a second and then back to Jake. "We suspected for a while. It was a test. And that's why we met in Rome."

"I guess you've taken care of the man."

"Not exactly," Russo said. "We can still use him for now."

Now Jake understood. This Malavita capo was as seasoned as an Agency officer. The guy obviously had street smarts, but also a strategic vision. "Where is he today?"

"Vibo Marina. A large boat with nearly five hundred dirtbags aboard is coming ashore. They passed through the Straights of Messina last night. The Italian government wants to settle these people in Calabria. My man is making sure that doesn't happen."

"How?" Alexandra asked.

Russo smiled. "Since you are German, you might not understand."

"I have nothing to do with the German government," Alexandra assured him.

"I understand. But the German government doesn't seem to get it. Until they do, and realize these people will simply become a burden to their society, then we will facilitate their transportation north. Italy cannot take all of these people. We don't even have jobs for Italians. Especially here in Calabria."

Carlos broke in. "This is a major problem that needs a solution. And we will not solve it here over lunch."

Alexandra swore under her breath in German.

"I understand German," Carlos said. "I have a lot of businesses there. And I feel for you and your people. But until the German government gets a clue, this is a logical solution."

"Is this why you have asked for my help again?" Jake asked.

Carlos shook his head. "No, no. This is an eventual threat, but there is a more imminent problem."

Before they could discuss that problem, their meals came—a tuna steak with fries. They ate in silence. Once they were done, Jake was the first to break in.

"I'm a little confused, Carlos," Jake said. "What exactly can I do to help you?"

"Chatter, as they say, is very high. The authorities believe a strike is imminent in Rome. But. . ."

"There's always a but," Jake said.

"The government in Rome seems to think that Russo's organization is the biggest threat," Carlos said. "They have tunnel vision."

"It is partially our fault," Russo said. "We have been successful in the past with. . ." He hesitated to find the right word. "Influence."

To them, Jake guessed, he meant assassination of political and business figures who got in the way of the Family.

"I see," Jake finally said. "And how can I help?"

"Both of you," Carlos said. "You both have contacts in the intelligence agencies. See which direction they might be taking. We need to make sure they see the trees in the forest."

Jake wasn't sure if the Spaniard was using the proper idiom, but he got the gist of his reasoning. Carlos needed them to poke and prod their contacts to see where they were looking. The guy had been nothing if not dependably straight with him over their short relationship, so he had no reason to suspect anything else this time. But Jake also had a healthy respect for potential bullshit. Or, in the case of Carlos, it was always possible that the man had a profit motive.

"What can we do to help?" Jake finally asked.

Carlos Gomez was scant on details, as usual, but heavy on the goals.

Then the billionaire said, "Russo will go back to Rome with you. The three of you will meet with a man who might know something about the plot against Italy."

"I wish you had told me this last night," Jake said. "It would have saved me a long drive."

"I'm sorry about that, Jake," Carlos said. "My jet was in Switzerland for routine maintenance. But it waits for you now at Lamezia Terme."

Jake had gotten a bit pampered traveling in the Spaniard's private jet in the past couple of years. The benefits of that mode of travel were significant—including his ability to bring as many weapons as necessary without worrying about airport security.

"All right," Jake said. "When's the meeting?"

"This evening," Carlos said.

Searing his gaze into the Malavita Capo, Jake said, "I would hope that only you know about this meeting from your organization."

"This is true," Russo said.

"You'll need to lose your security, then," Jake said.

"My security?"

Jake pointed out four men set up at various locations outside of the restaurant, describing each in detail.

Alexandra said, "And you'll need to have one of your people talk to a fat man back at the city parking lot who tried to shake us down."

"As soon as we mentioned your name, he backed off," Jake said.

"He won't bother you again," Russo assured them.

"No need to kill him or break his legs," Alexandra said. "Just a talk."

"Of course."

After agreeing on a time to meet at the airport, Jake got up and shook both of their hands.

Before they could leave, Carlos said, "There will be extra in your compensation this time. For the little girl."

Jake and Alexandra both thanked the billionaire and then drifted out to the street. Although it was sunny out, there was already a chill in the air, as if December was trying to creep in before its time.

Neither of them said a word for a while, knowing they were being watched. Finally, Jake stopped and pulled Alexandra to him, kissing her quickly on the lips. Then, as he hugged her, he whispered into her ear. "Are you all right going along with this case?"

"Why wouldn't I be? Have I not changed enough diapers?"

He smiled and spanked her ass playfully. Then they wandered back to their Fiat.

3

Athens, Greece

Elisa Murici sat at a small café in a western slum of the city, in an area of the capital that most tourists would never see. What had been nearly pure white buildings at some point, had been transformed into a dull charcoal and that canvas was riddled with enough graffiti to make her wonder who owned the spray paint distribution in the city. Whoever it was had to be rich, she guessed. The truth was, though, the graffiti might have been the only thing holding some of the buildings up. And some of the artwork was stunning. She glanced at her cell phone as if checking her status on social media, but she was actually on her camera viewing the scene behind her. Her target lived across the street, but she had been scrutinized by a man who entered the café a few minutes ago. When she realized he was simply there for a quick coffee and could have merely been admiring her as a woman, she checked on her appearance. Although she was Italian, her hair was normally blonde compliments of her Czech mother, she had died it recently to black. But she couldn't cover up her high cheek bones.

Her phone suddenly buzzed and she saw the fake picture of her contact. She picked up, making sure not to speak too loudly here in Italian. She went through the standard niceties, as if she were simply talking with a sister or brother. But this was her boss at the Italian External Intelligence and Security Agency. *Agenzia informazioni e sicurezza sterna* or AISE, was responsible for state security outside of Italy, much like the CIA operated outside of America.

"Si," Elisa said into her phone.

"We need a progress report," her boss said.

She checked her watch and realized she was a couple of hours late. "There's nothing to report."

AISE had gotten chatter about a potential bomb maker living in this area of Athens. The man was a naturalized Greek citizen who had come to the city during the major immigration influx following the Iraq War. They suspected he had learned bomb building during that conflict and had become a free agent. Which is why Elisa was sitting on the man.

"We got word that Zamir has booked passage on the Grimaldi Line ferry tonight at seventeen hundred, from Patras to Brindisi."

"How? He hasn't left his apartment."

"He used his current disposable phone."

That was strange and out of character for this man, who had been extremely careful with his communications. The man bought a new phone almost daily.

"That doesn't seem strange to you?" she asked.

"Thank God every one of the bastards make mistakes. Just follow him to Italy."

"Yes, sir. But what happens once he reaches Italy?" Officially they were not supposed to work on Italian soil. That was the purview of AISI, the Internal Information and Security Agency, the equivalent of the American FBI.

"I'm working on a special arrangement."

"You recall what happened last time in Sicily," she reminded him. Elisa had worked on Italian soil without proper authorization and it had caused a firestorm of activity. But her results had made things right. Deep down, she knew that her friend Jake Adams had applied pressure through his contacts.

"Let me worry about your authorization," he said sternly. Then he hung up.

Her phone went back to camera mode and she glanced at her own concerned face. She still wasn't used to the black hair. Or the curls.

Now what? She checked her watch again and realized Zamir would have to be on the move soon if he wanted to get to Patras in time to catch the ferry. She had two options. She could check out of her hotel and get to Patras on her own, or she could check out and follow Zamir to the ferry terminal. But that was risky. Over the past week she had been able to change her appearance and go undetected. She needed to maintain her cover. No, the best option was to beat Zamir to the ferry. Her only concern was if this was a ruse to throw her off. She would be stuck on a damn ferry back to Italy, while he traveled across the border into Albania or Macedonia.

Did she have a choice? Not really. She got up and started to wander back toward her hotel. Elisa barely made it a few steps when Zamir came out of his apartment carrying a bag over his shoulder. He had changed his appearance, though. Instead of dark scraggly hair nearly to his shoulders, he had cut off all of his hair to within a centimeter of his scalp. His clothes were also different, changing from jeans and a T-shirt into black slacks and a leather jacket. Zamir got into a taxi and it almost immediately drove off. She memorized the license plate.

Now she picked up her pace. While she hiked to her hotel a couple blocks away, she texted the taxi license plate to her people.

It took her just fifteen minutes to gather her bag and check out of the hotel. Then she got into her rental car and hurried toward Patras, which was more than 200 kilometers to the west. If she pushed it, she could make that in three hours.

4

Tropea, Italy

After getting back from lunch with the Spaniard, Jake struggled with what to do. A simple meeting in Rome had nearly gotten he and Alexandra killed, and he sure as hell didn't want his little Emma raised by someone else. He had already lost more than 20 years with his son, who had been raised by his ex-girlfriend's sister. Who would take over Emma? They hadn't even discussed that. His siblings lived in Montana. Her relatives lived in northern Germany. But her father was dead and her mother in a memory care home. She had no siblings. Only distant cousins like Monica.

Jake sat on the edge of his bed and checked out the clothes he had rolled up, along with the two Glocks and multiple magazines of 9mm jacketed hollow points. Alexandra was rummaging in the walk-in closet. He wasn't sure she was going to like what he had to say, but he had to say it anyway.

"Alexandra," Jake said.

She poked her head out of the closet. "Yeah."

"I think you should sit this one out."

Now she stepped out, her hands on her hips. "Why do you say that?"

"I don't know. I thought we were going to slow down a bit now that Emma was in our life."

She glared at him like a cat looking for an opportunity to attack. Then she pointed at him and said, "I've been sitting on my fat ass for the past year, growing like a monster. Then I push out another human and spend day and night feeding her and cleaning her shit diapers, and you don't think I need a little time away from that?"

Jake got up from the bed and stepped a little closer, but not within striking distance. He wasn't entirely crazy. "It's not like we're going to Club Med. This is an op."

"Look around, Jake. We damn near live in Club Med. It doesn't get any more sedate than this."

"I know. But after last night. . ."

"I've been telling you for years that you're a shit magnet, Jake."

True. She had.

"I mean, only you could turn a wedding into a damn riot."

She was still talking about her cousin's wedding in Germany three years ago. "That wasn't my fault," he said. "The guy said that American football was a pussy sport. I simply disagreed. Vehemently."

"You broke his jaw," she said. "And then you injured three of his friends."

"But I didn't touch the groom."

"True. But the rest of the wedding party was destroyed."

"Can we get back to the point? Emma needs her mother."

"She needs her father also."

He couldn't argue that point. "What if something happens to the both of us? We haven't even discussed who will raise her."

"Your parents are dead. My father is dead, and my mother is literally losing her mind. She is perhaps a year away from not even knowing me. What about your side?"

"As you know, they're both in Montana."

"Beautiful country."

"True. But I'm not sure who would be best for Emma. Victor's life is hectic, and as far as I know, Jessica is. . .well, she's Jessica."

"She's a great woman," Alexandra said.

"You've only met her once."

"That was enough to know."

"She's staunchly independent. Like an old cowgirl."

"Not old."

"Old in cowgirl years." Jake waved his hand. "All right. You can go with me."

Alexandra smiled. "I wasn't giving you a choice. My cousin Monica was part of the Polizei anti-terrorism task force, so I'm sure she can handle Emma."

Jake had to admit that Monica had a way with the baby. He was suspecting some sort of mind altering drugs, but his brain seemed to vector in odd directions since Emma's birth.

"Are you almost ready?" Jake asked. "We need to get to Lamezia."

"You can't wait to ride on that Gulfstream."

"They have my favorite rum."

"We have your favorite rum."

"It's not the same. Anyway, let's leave in fifteen."

"No problem."

Jake left her in the bedroom. He wandered out into the kitchen and to the living room. Monica was sleeping on the sofa with the baby monitor on the table next to her. She raised an eye lid as Jake entered.

"Are you heading out?" Monica asked.

"In a few minutes," he said. "Thanks again for your help and support."

"It's not a problem. I love Emma. And you know that I adore Alexandra."

He nodded and smiled before going out through the sliding glass door to the terrace overlooking the sea. The sky was swirling with clouds. A front was coming in, he guessed.

Jake took out his phone and punched in a number from memory.

A man answered. "Do you know how early it is here on the east coast?"

Of course, he did. "Come on, Kurt. You can't sleep anyway."

Kurt Jenkins was formerly Director of the CIA, but he had been retired now for a couple of years. Yet, he still had pull in the Agency and other parts of government, from the State Department to Defense.

"You know me too well, Jake. What the hell can I do for you this time?"

"You can start by not being such a dick."

"Sorry, I'm only on my third cappuccino."

Jake explained what had happened the night before and that he and Alexandra would be heading to Rome to look into some terrorist chatter.

"You hear anything imminent coming to the Eternal City?"

"I'm out of the game Jake," Kurt said. "I don't even get calls to play golf anymore."

"Bullshit. I heard you were working for the same network as us."

"Who told you. . .never mind. Considering General Graves kept some of our nation's most closely-held secrets, he has loose lips."

"I didn't say it was Tom." But it was General Tom Graves.

"All right. I'll see what we've got on this end. You better get going if you want to catch that flight in Lamezia Terme."

Jake laughed and shook his head. Out of the game, his ass. Kurt was still dialed in. He clicked off the call and shoved his phone into his pocket.

He gazed out again at the sea and up the coast toward Rome. Jake wasn't sure what was going on, but that never stopped him in the past. As always, he thought, the case would reveal itself.

Now he went back inside and gathered his bag and weapons. He and Alexandra kissed a sleeping baby before piling into their little beat up Fiat and driving toward the airport in Lamezia Terme.

5

Geneva, Switzerland

Dark clouds swirled over the city, with rain threatening, as darkness started to shroud the western suburb of Vernier.

This city on the western edge of Lake Geneva didn't really have slums, but there were a few areas of the city where most felt unsafe to travel at night. Le Lignon, a massive housing development built in the 60s and 70s near the Geneva Airport, was one of those places—even for the *Bundesamt für Polizei*, or Federal Office of Police.

Derrick Konrad was officially still part of the Swiss Polizei, but he had been assigned to an INTERPOL task force six months ago, and was charged with uncovering any potential threat to Switzerland. He had put a particular apartment under surveillance two weeks ago, and felt they had enough evidence against those inside to finally authorize a raid. Konrad had once been a member of the Swiss Army Special Forces before transitioning to civilian law enforcement nearly ten years ago. He was a tall, blond man of Germanic heritage—his family originally Prussian. Perhaps a little overweight compared to his days in the Army, he was still fit enough, he reasoned.

Their surveillance included two twelve-hour shifts of two-man teams, where they sat two stories above their target apartment on the tenth floor. This apartment complex included twenty stories of connecting buildings zigzagging through a park-like setting. Since their section of the building was at a forty-five-degree angle from that of their target, it gave them a direct view into the subject's apartment. That is, when they actually pulled their shades. But Konrad and his team had other methods of surveillance, including audio, infra-red, and communications intercepts. They not only knew who these people spoke with on the phone, but what channels they watched on their television.

"What are they watching on the television?" Konrad asked his associate, Holgar, a younger man in his late twenties.

"Same as before. Music videos. Arab rap."

"For all of their fundamental ramblings, they sure like the more decadent things in life," Konrad said. "They drink more than the local Swiss. And go to dance clubs like it's the Nineties."

"Nobody goes to discos anymore, Derrick," his associate said. "At least not to find new women."

This was news to him. "Why not?"

"They're too busy hooking up on apps," Holgar said. "If they're having sex at all. The Swiss are becoming pandas. If we keep failing to breed, we will become extinct."

Konrad nodded agreement. This was a problem across Europe. The normally indigenous people had a negative birth rate, while the immigrants were breeding like rabbits. "That's the only reason our governments allow so many people in. We don't have enough people to work in the factories."

"Everything is produced in China anyway."

The radio burst to life and a man said, "We have approval to move on the apartment."

Konrad keyed the talk button and said, "Roger that. ETA for SWAT?"

"En route. Ten to arrive. Ten to get in place. Do you have eyes on the subjects?"

"Yes, sir. They're drinking beer and watching videos on the television."

"Roger that. Hold tight and continue to monitor."

No shit! Konrad really wanted to be in on the raid, but he understood his current role. He would let those with body armor kick in the door. But he sure as hell wanted access to everything found inside. Electronic surveillance was important, but it didn't compare with hands on evidence.

As they waited for the strike team, Konrad ran everything through his mind. Three men hung out at the apartment, but only two were on the actual lease. The other man was the one they really needed. And he was a wildcard. The two on the lease were both former Syrian nationals. This third man? Unknown. But they assumed he too was of Syrian nationality. Konrad could understand Arabic, but he was not an expert with the Syrian dialect. Yet, their dialect expert had confirmed his nationality.

Konrad went to a table with the plans for the building spread out. Days ago they had confirmed how a potential raid would be conducted. Because of the building structure, all they needed to do was cut off the corridor, the stairwells on each side, and the bank of elevators. The men had a balcony, but they would be crazy to jump from the tenth floor. And, only three levels of the twenty stories had balconies, so they couldn't go up or down by dropping from one floor to the next. No, they had them cold.

"Derrick, we might have a problem," his associate said.

Konrad hurried back to the monitor. "What is it?"

"Only the two residents are in the living room."

"What about our mystery man?"

"I don't know. He got up a few minutes ago and went to the kitchen."

Picking up his binoculars, Konrad checked the balcony. No activity. Luckily, on this evening, they had left their shade open. So he could see the glow of the TV.

"Shit," Konrad said. "Loop back the video and audio." Holgar didn't understand Arabic, so perhaps he had missed something. "Stop there." He picked up the headset and listened as the video ran.

"What is it?" His associate tapped his foot and bit his nails.

"Shit, shit, shit." Konrad picked up the radio and keyed in to speak with the assault leader. "Missing one man. He's on the move out the building."

"We're already in the building," came a voice over the radio. "We're moving in."

"Crap." He handed the radio to his associate. "I'm going after our mystery man." Then he quickly put in an ear bud comm unit and slung his coat on, tucking it behind his 9mm Sig Sauer on his right hip.

"I should go with you."

"No, you need to be their eyes on the raid." Konrad gave his partner an uplifted jaw and hurried out the door.

Luckily, he had memorized the layout of the building. If he hurried, he could rush out the end of the complex and catch his target before he got on the tram. He knew that none of the three owned a car, so public transportation was their only option.

As Konrad ran down the corridor, he said into his mic, "Heading to the Avanchet tram stop."

He couldn't hear if anyone acknowledged his report. But he kept running. When he reached the bank of elevators in his building, he got lucky and rushed in, hitting the ground floor button. He got off and headed outside into a light drizzle. Darkness now was nearly complete, with the few lights in the courtyard having come to life.

There, he thought. He could see the man about one hundred meters across the park moving toward the tram line. He was on the phone.

Konrad said into his mic. "Who is our mystery man talking with?"

"What's he saying?"

"I don't know."

Damn it! He kept his distance, making sure not to be seen by hanging close to the shrubs and trees near the building.

Now he listened to the raid as it unfolded, his eyes concentrating on how his mystery man reacted to that. Suddenly the man, still on the phone, swiveled around and glanced up at his building. Konrad kept walking slowly, but he made sure to cover his gun now with his jacket.

"Speak to me," Konrad whispered into his mic.

"They took the men without incident," his associate said. "Do you have the third man?"

"So far. But he just got off the phone and shoved it into his pocket. I need you to translate his conversation and get back to me immediately. We have to assume he knows about the raid."

"Will do, Derrick."

He followed the man to the tram stop and tried his best not to stare at the Syrian. His target got on the tram and headed toward downtown Geneva. The Syrian was in the middle and Konrad was in the very back of the tram. He asked his Polizei contact for direction, but none came immediately. Should he take this man now? Or would the man lead him to someone else?

It didn't matter. He never got the authorization to arrest this guy. For all they knew, this wasn't even their mystery man tied to that apartment. But Konrad knew the truth. It was him. He had observed him for days from their post in the apartment complex. Other local Polizei detectives had even followed him to various locations around the city. But to this point he had never done anything to warrant an arrest.

Once the tram reached downtown Geneva, the suspect got off at the main train station and went in directly to buy a ticket. But to which destination. Konrad had watched the man use cash for the transaction before wandering toward the platforms.

Pulling his INTERPOL identification, Konrad asked the ticket agent the destination of the Syrian. Zurich. He bought a ticket on the same train and then wandered through the terminal making a few phone calls. First, he called his boss at INTERPOL and told him where he was going. Then he called his associate's private phone instead of transmitting it across his comm unit.

"I'm following our mystery man to Zurich on the next train," Konrad said. "What did they find at the raid?"

"Unauthorized weapons and bomb-making materials. But no explosives."

"That would come," Konrad said. "Have the men said anything?"

His associate laughed. "They're talking like little school girls. They both claim that the third man owned all the guns and the bomb materials."

"Of course. They were giving him a place to stay."

"Right. What will you do?"

"Heading to Zurich. "I'll pick up a new partner there."

"It's been great working with you, Derrick."

"Same to you."

"Take care."

Konrad simply nodded and clicked off the call, shoving his phone into his pocket. Then he went to his train and got into the first-class car.

6

Rome, Italy

After a nice leisurely flight from Lamezia Terme to Rome Ciampino Airport, the alternative to the busy Fiumicino International Airport, the Spaniard's people had a rental car available for Jake, Alexandra and Sergio Russo. It was a ubiquitous Fiat Tipo with the turbo diesel.

Jake drove toward the center of Rome, with Russo in the front passenger seat giving him directions to their meeting location. Alexandra sat quietly in the back seat behind Jake.

"What do you know about this guy we're meeting tonight?" Jake asked Russo.

"He's a cousin."

"A first cousin?"

"We don't care about first or second or third," Russo said. "Blood is blood."

Fair enough. "Do you trust him?"

Russo looked at Jake as if he had asked the most ignorant question possible. "He's my cousin. I trust him with my life."

"Do you know what kind of information he has?" Alexandra asked from the back seat.

Shaking his head, Russo said, "No. He said it was something big. Something about speculation of attack of Roma."

"Why not drop a dime to the Polizia?" Jake asked, already knowing the answer. The Malavita didn't cooperate with the police. But they did control certain aspects of the force.

"You're a funny man, Jake."

"It's part of his charm," Alexandra explained.

Jake shrugged. "Well, there is such a thing as an anonymous tip."

By now they were in the downtown area, first passing the Colosseum and then cutting past the Piazza

Venezia. Then Jake turned right down the Via del Corso, a main shopping street that was like the spine of the city. His mind drifted back to the many times he had been here with Toni Contardo over the years, while she was assigned here with the Agency. From Via del Corso they could veer off in any direction to see landmarks like the Trevi Fountain, the Spanish Steps, or the Pantheon.

"Left, Jake," Russo said.

Jake turned and soon saw that the road was blocked ahead.

"Park anywhere," Russo said.

Jake pulled in behind a line of cars and shut down the engine. "Where from here?"

"We just passed it."

Twisting around, Jake saw only a small church. "We're meeting there?"

"Yes. My cousin is a priest." Russo hesitated. "What? You think the whole family is part of the Malavita?"

"Maybe," Jake mumbled.

Russo smiled. "Most of us are. Let's go."

Of the thousand churches in Rome, this one wouldn't make the top 100, Jake guessed. It was a mini-Gothic structure with limited stained glass and a subdued alter. It was cold and dank and Jake thought that parishioners would need a down jacket in the summer to sit through an hour mass. A copula to the right held a small statue of some saint, with a bank of small white candles lit—perhaps more for warmth than prayer.

As the three of them wandered down the center aisle, Jake thought about a few other meetings he had taken in churches over the years. A couple had turned into major shoot outs, so he remained vigilant despite the sanctity of the setting.

When they got near the first row of pews, a priest came from behind the alter. He was a short, dumpy man with terminal baldness—genes that would not be passed on through progeny.

"Your cousin?" Jake whispered.

"Si."

The priest met his cousin and they kissed on both cheeks. Then Russo introduced the priest to Jake and Alexandra. Instead of the familiar greeting, the priest kept it to a simple handshake with Jake. Alexandra got the full treatment.

"Please sit," the priest said.

The three of them did that, while the padre remained standing.

"What do you have for us?" Jake asked, letting the priest know this wasn't a social visit.

The priest seemed a bit put off by Jake's brusque attitude. Finally, he said, "I need to frame this in a hypothetical situation."

Jake understood this. The good priest had gotten his information from confessional, and he didn't want to breech his trust with his parishioner. So Jake gave the man a little leash and waited patiently.

"Let's say a person knows something that could harm a lot of people," the priest said. "A vow is important, but the lives of the innocent are more so. We cannot allow death and destruction. Especially not in Roma."

Thank God, Jake thought. A practical priest. "Go on."

"A woman dates a man who does not have her best interest at heart."

Jake considered this holy man's English and his talking in riddles, and came to the conclusion he was quite well educated and intelligent. He had found this to be true of most priests he had come across over the years.

"What does this man have planned?" Russo asked his cousin. This sounded more like a demand than a request.

"This is difficult for me," the priest said.

The three of them were silent now. Waiting.

Finally, the priest said, "They plan to strike a number of locations around the city simultaneously."

"Muslim terrorists?" Russo asked.

The priest shook his head. "She said her boyfriend was a Muslim, but not a strict Muslim. I asked."

Jake said, "But. . ."

"The targets are not specifically religious," the priest said.

"You know the targets?" Jake asked.

"No. And she does not either. It's just what her friend said."

So, Jake surmised, this boyfriend was either all bluster to impress the girl, or he had enough sense not to divulge all of the plot. Still, this could be significant. Although many sites in Rome were not religious in nature, like the Colosseum, the city as a whole was host to more Catholic sites per square mile than any other on earth. "We need names," Jake said.

The priest shook his head.

Russo stood up and got in his cousin's face. Although Jake considered himself mostly fluent in Italian now, much that came out of the Malavita man's mouth was filled with Calabrese slang. Luckily that's where Jake learned most of the language, so he picked up enough to know that Russo was laying it on thick with his cousin. He was playing the role of Malavita capo now. And Jake guessed the man was good at his job.

"I only know the name of the young woman," the priest finally said, the fear of God riddled across his face. "Marisa Carioti. She lives just three blocks from here with another young woman from the church." The priest gave them the address. "She works at the Gatto Nero Ristorante near the Pantheon. She might be working now."

"Do you have a picture of her?" Jake asked.

The priest shook his head. "Afraid not."

Jake thanked the priest and headed for the front with Alexandra on his side. Russo stayed behind, his hands on the shoulders of his cousin. Then the two of them kissed and Russo followed them out.

"You were quiet back there," Jake said to Alexandra once they got outside.

"I have a problem with the whole sanctity of confession," she said. "I understand it in the abstract. I'm just glad this priest has the sense to say something to possibly save lives. My faith in humanity could be on the rise."

She hadn't been out in the field with Jake in a while, he thought. He guessed her feelings might have been due to her recent motherhood. Although she had been reared as a Catholic in Germany, Jake couldn't remember a time when she had attended mass. The same could be said of Jake also, though. But they had discussed the confessional in the past. She couldn't understand why she couldn't simply pray to God on her own, confessing her sins in the process, without an earthly vessel to intercede. Why not cut out the middle man?

The three of them walked quietly down the street toward the address for the young woman. Jake guessed this young woman might be pissed off that the priest betrayed her. "Let's not mention the priest," Jake said.

"How else can we justify our questioning of her?" Alexandra asked.

Jake smiled. "My guess is that she didn't just open up to her priest. Who does a young girl usually confide in?"

Russo took this. "Her girlfriends."

"Correct."

They found the apartment and climbed up to the first floor through a dark stairwell. As they entered the corridor, it was obvious that something wasn't right. It was in total darkness.

Instinctively, Jake drew his gun and moved forward as his eyes adjusted to the blackness. He checked the door numbers and saw that the woman's apartment would be the next one ahead on the left. A sliver of light seeped out to the corridor.

Slowly he moved to the edge of the door and listened. But there was no sound. His heart raced, unsure of what he would find inside. With his left hand, he shoved the door open all the way. More light shone out to the corridor.

He glanced at Alexandra and Russo, who had not drawn their weapons. Maybe he was being overcautious. With one swift motion, he stepped into the apartment and swept his gun from one side of the room to the other.

Shit! Lying face down in the center of the room, blood seeping from several cuts through a white T-shirt, was a young woman in her underwear. Jake could see the kitchen area, but he needed to clear the back bedrooms. He pointed to the woman on the floor for

Alexandra to check out while he covered them. By now Alexandra had her gun out and she knelt to check for a pulse. She shook her head and then got up, moving in close behind Jake as the two of them stepped gently toward the bedrooms.

Jake clicked on a light and cleared the first bedroom. Then they went to the far back bedroom and cleared that one. But whoever had stabbed this woman had gone.

When they got back to the living room, Russo was down on his knees looking at the woman.

"What do you see?" Jake asked.

"A knife," Russo said. "A big knife, I think. I count at least five stab wounds."

A large puddle of blood surrounded the torso of the woman.

"Probably more on the other side," Jake said. He gently rolled the body over and pulled the long black hair from the dead woman's face. He was right. There was one more stab wound in her chest between her smallish breasts. He turned to Alexandra. "Could you check for a purse and ID?"

Alexandra nodded and wandered through the apartment. Moments later she came back with a brown leather purse and pulled out a phone with an ID and credit cards. She pulled out a driver's license and compared it with the woman. "This isn't Marisa Carioti," she said. "It's the roommate. Elena Lombardo. Age twenty-two."

"Damn it," Jake said, setting the woman back into her original position. "Let's go. We need to get to the restaurant pronto."

The three of them rushed out of the apartment.

7

The Gatto Nero Ristorante sat on the corner of two streets a couple of blocks from the Pantheon, one of Rome's most famous ancient landmarks.

Alexandra was driving now, and she had parked the Fiat with a view of the restaurant ahead, and about a block beyond that a lightly armored military vehicle with two personnel armed with submachine guns stood guard.

Jake reached for the door handle and stopped. "Keep the car running. Let me get the girl alone."

"I can go with you," Russo said.

"I don't want to scare the crap out of her," Jake said. "Let's not mention her roommate."

He got out without a response from the others and wandered toward the front of the restaurant. Before he left the girl's apartment, he had found a couple of photos of Marisa framed. So at least he would be able to pick her out of the wait staff.

The restaurant was packed. Jake scanned the room and saw various waiters and waitresses moving about from table to table. Finally, in the far back, he saw Marisa taking the orders of a large group.

This would take a delicate approach, Jake thought. How could he convince her to come with him without freaking her out?

As he approached her, he was suddenly shoved from behind as a man passed him.

The young waitress turned in shock to see the man before her.

When Jake saw the gun at the man's leg, he rushed forward just as the other man was raising the gun toward Marisa.

Jake struck the man in the right kidney, buckling him to the ground. People started to scream and dive for cover.

Marisa stood in shock.

Twisting and snapping a kick, Jake knocked the gunman into a metal chair and under a table.

Then came a shot from behind him. Jake drew his gun and stepped in front of Marisa.

More shots from the front entrance.

Jake aimed and shot three times, hitting the guy center mass.

Marisa screamed and Jake turned to see the first gunman collecting his gun and aiming at her.

Jake shot three more times, hitting the man twice in the chest and once in the mouth.

More people screamed.

"Come with me or you will die," Jake said in Italian to Marisa.

She nodded, but he could tell she was frozen in shock.

Jake grasped her hand and pulled her toward the front door. Into his mic Jake said, "A little help. Is the front clear?"

"On the way," Alexandra said, "but the security from the Pantheon are on the way."

"Cut down the front of the building," Jake said.

As Jake rounded the front door, he heard a car peeling tires and speeding down the street.

Alexandra pulled up and Jake opened the back door, shoving Marisa inside and following her. "Follow that car," Jake instructed.

"Already on it," Alexandra said. She burned rubber as she sped away.

They were a block behind the other car, which happened to be another dark Audi like the one that had chased them the other night.

Alexandra looked at Jake in the rearview mirror. "What the hell happened?"

"They came for Marisa," Jake said. Then he looked to his right and saw that the young woman was shaking and in shock.

"We can't catch that Audi," Alexandra said. "It's too fast."

Jake grasped Marisa's arm and said, "Who are these people? And why do they want you dead?"

Marisa simply shrugged.

He hated to do this, but he pulled out his phone and brought up a picture of her roommate. "Do you want to end up like this?"

The young woman's eyes got wide. "Elena?"

Jake took the phone back and shoved it into his pocket. "That's right. She was butchered in your apartment. I'm guessing they were looking for you, which is why we came to find you."

Her eyes darted to the right to avoid Jake's intense gaze. Then the car took a sharp turn to the right and

Marisa landed in Jake's arms. When this happened, Marisa finally broke down and cried, hugging Jake like a scared child. Jake glanced to the front and saw Alexandra in the rearview mirror nodding her approval. He guessed she had made that turn sharper than necessary.

Despite their fast speed, Jake could look ahead and see that the Audi had lost them. Sirens echoed throughout this area of Rome now, seeming to come from every direction.

Once Alexandra had the car cruising at a relatively normal pace and Marisa had time to settle down, Jake backed away slightly and said, "Do you know why these men are trying to kill you?"

She said nothing at first, but her facial contortion said everything to Jake. She knew.

"You knew the men who tried to kill you at the restaurant," Jake stated.

Finally, she said, "The close man was my old boyfriend. The man you killed at the door was his friend."

"And the driver of the car?" he asked.

"If I had to guess, I would say friends of my old boyfriend. They are roommates."

"What's the address?"

She said nothing.

Jake pushed her. "They will continue to try to kill you. And you know why. Because your dumbass ex-boyfriend couldn't keep his mouth shut about his plans. Am I right?"

"How do you know this?" Marisa asked.

"Because dumbass boyfriends have been boasting about future conquests since Biblical times. Humans can't help themselves."

Marisa still had an anguished expression, but it seemed to have become a bit more manageable. Perhaps Jake was getting through to her.

Jake got her to give up the address where her old boyfriend lived. The two men would only be there long enough to grab their stuff and leave, he guessed. So they had to hurry. Russo directed Alexandra to the address. While they worked on getting there, Jake first made sure he had a full magazine in his gun. These men would not come easily. But he also knew he needed to interrogate at least one of them.

"Do you have names and nationalities of the men?" Jake asked.

Marisa shook her head. "Just first names. My old boyfriend was a Syrian. The man you shot at the front door was from Jordan."

"And the other two?"

"One is a Turk, but the other is Italian. The apartment is his."

She gave Jake the first names, but that wouldn't really help much right now. Eventually, he would be able to look into the Italian's background—assuming it mattered. For now, though, they just needed to take these two men alive. That was the only way to extract intel. To discover the plot against Rome.

8

Crotone, Italy

The drive from the Amalfi Coast south to Calabria had been enjoyable, yet arduous for Antonio Baroni. Since he was in his early 50s, he guessed his tiredness was understandable. He could see that in his math. With all the factors included—age, distance driven, atmospheric conditions, road construction, and crazy Italian drivers—factored with things like cappuccino per hour and the number of autostrada stops for relief, and his condition was completely known.

He swished his black marker on the whiteboard trying to develop a more interesting equation—one which could vault him out of obscurity. Baroni had until recently been a professor of advanced mathematics and physics at the Crotone Institute of Technology, a prestigious school with links to his hero Pythagoras, who had taught there before Christ had been born. To just walk the same cobblestone streets as Pythagoras was a profound accomplishment. Deep down he knew he wasn't worthy to be uttered in the same breath as that great man, but some had done so years ago. Of course, that was when he was a promising young mathematician. Now they had nearly thrown him to the wolves. Officially he had retired. Unofficially, he had been forced to acquiesce to their will.

There was a light knock on his office door but he didn't turn to see who was there. He knew it could have only been his most trusted advisor, a former student and protégé, Marco.

His man opened the door and peered around the edge. Marco was a handsome, fit man in his late twenties. "Sir?"

Baroni waved the man in, and then turned again to his whiteboard in deep contemplation. "What is it?"

Marco cleared his throat. "We have a problem in Rome."

"What kind of problem?"

"Two of our men were killed in a shoot-out."

Baroni swiveled around quickly. "What? How? Why?"

"We don't know the details yet. Our Italian friend there spoke with his contact. He contacted me."

That was how Baroni had built his organization, from scratch with concentric layers of insulation, keeping him at least one level away from the frontline workers.

"Who did we lose?" Baroni asked.

"A Syrian and Jordanian," Marco said.

Not a problem, he thought. That left the Italian and the Turk in that cell. And the Italian was resourceful. He would easily find replacements. Besides, he glanced to the largest of his whiteboards, which contained his grand plan for Italy, they were simply his eyes in Roma. The fingers, the hands and the arms were coming to play soon. And the eyes had nearly finished their work.

But something was bothering Baroni. "Did the Polizia or the Carabinieri kill them?"

"No, sir. They said it was just one man."

"The man from the Malavita?"

"No, no. The man who met the man from the Malavita the other night in Rome."

"Who is this man?"

Marco shook his head. "We don't know, sir."

Baroni pointed to the large whiteboard. "Do you see that board, Marco?"

His man nodded agreement.

"Do you see this unknown factor anywhere in that equation?"

"No, sir."

"I don't either. We can't have unknown variables mucking up our beautiful equation. Can we?"

"Of course not."

"Agreed. Have our Italian friend in Roma hire anyone he needs to eliminate that unknown variable."

Marco nodded.

"That will be all," Baroni said.

But Marco stood for a moment, his eyes concentrating on the smaller whiteboard, the one his boss had been contemplating when he entered the office.

"What's the matter, Marco?"

"If I may, your problem. If X is garlic, you might consider increasing that level. Minestrone can always use more garlic."

Baroni glanced at his whiteboard as his man Marco exited the room. He would consider that. Soup, like everything else in life, required the perfect level of ingredients. Too much of one thing could throw the entire brine into disarray. Again he turned his attention on his grand scheme whiteboard. Who was this unknown variable? And what were the odds of this one man changing the outcome of his equation?

9

Rome, Italy

Before going to the apartment of the Italian and the Turk, Jake directed Alexandra to another location, a hotel just outside the walls of the Vatican, where he checked in under his Austrian persona and dropped the scared Italian woman off, leaving Russo to watch her.

Now, he sat in the front passenger seat of the Fiat in a quiet neighborhood on Rome's north side.

Alexandra kept the car running, her eyes concentrating on the apartment building less than a block away. "That's got to be their Audi," she said.

"I agree," Jake said.

"How do you want to play this?"

"Alone," he said. "I can handle these two dirtbags."

"What if Marisa is wrong, and they have more men?"

She had a point. But he also knew that she was a bit rusty from her time off with maternity. Would she bounce back to her old self? Or was this simply his problem, not wanting either of them to get killed or injured? Their daughter needed at least one of them to survive, and now Jake was questioning his line of work.

He pulled out his phone and punched in a number without regard for the time difference. Then he waited.

"Who are you calling?" she asked.

"Old friends."

The former Director of the CIA, Kurt Jenkins, came on the line and rattled off a list of crap he had heard was going down in Rome. "What the hell is going on there?"

Jake shook his head. "You know how it goes. Shit happens, Kurt."

"Well the Agency is pissed," Kurt said. "Something about two dead men in a restaurant near the Pantheon."

Jake explained the situation with the woman he had stashed in the hotel and the lead she gave him. "I'm guessing the Agency is only pissed because I didn't give them a heads up."

"That's right," Kurt said. "They get their feelings hurt when a former officer knows more than their own officers and agents in the field."

"Now days they're all a bunch of Harvard educated assholes who try to intellectualize the mind of radicals," Jake said. "You can't reason with radicals, Kurt. You can only kill them. They need to hire more ex-military."

"The new Director is working on that," Kurt assured Jake. "But it takes time to hire and train these people." His old friend hesitated. "What do you need from me?"

Jake glanced at Alexandra, who seemed more than a little concerned with his conversation. "I need the Agency to pick up and protect this woman. At least until I can track down all of these assholes who want her dead."

"Roger that. Where do you have her holed up?"

He thought for a moment and realized he didn't want the Agency to know too much too soon. Nor did he want them to mess with his Malavita contact, Sergio Russo.

"I'll get back with you in about an hour," Jake finally said. Then he cut the call short before Kurt Jenkins could respond.

"Will they help?" she asked.

"Eventually."

"But you don't want them learning what she knows yet."

"That's right. I need to talk with these assholes before they bolt." He made sure he had easy access to his Glock as he opened the door and got out.

Alexandra got out and rushed up to Jake.

"You should stay at the car," Jake said.

"Right. You want me to go to the kitchen and make you strudel?"

"That's not it," he said. "But I am a little hungry."

She hit his arm. "We're going to play drunken girlfriend," Alexandra demanded.

Damn it. He hated drunken girlfriend. But she was right. The neighbors would remember a drunken girl more than an imposing man.

So they wandered down the street with Alexandra staggering and hanging on to Jake's left side to keep from falling over.

Once they got into the apartment building, they climbed to the first floor and drew their guns, making their way down the corridor to the last apartment on the right.

Just as they were about to kick in the door, it swung open and a man with dark hair looked surprised.

Jake shoved his gun at the man and said in Italian, "Drop the bag and back up."

The man turned his head and started to say something, but Jake punched the man with his left fist, knocking the man to his knees. Jake shoved his right foot into the man's chest, taking his breath away. When the second man appeared, Jake started to raise his gun and he heard one shot. The man across the room crumpled to the floor with a great crash.

Jake turned to see Alexandra pointing her gun to his left.

"I had to shoot," she said.

"Help me with him," Jake said. "Bring his bag."

She slung the man's bag over her shoulder and helped Jake lift the man from the floor. Then together the two of them dragged the man out the door and down the corridor. After her shot, Jake expected to see curious neighbors gawking out their doors. But this wasn't that kind of neighborhood. This was a keep your damn mouth shut kind of place.

On the ground floor, Jake held the man while Alexandra ran and got the car. He took the time to check the guy for weapons, finding a 9mm CZ-75, Jake's old weapon of choice, along with two knifes. He stuffed those into the guy's duffle bag. When the guy struggled to get away, Jake elbowed the guy in the jaw, nearly knocking the man out.

Moments later Alexandra pulled up and Jake hauled the groggy man into the back seat. Then Alexandra took off at a slow pace.

Once they got down the road and away from the apartment, Jake slapped the man across the face, startling him back to life. Jake had assumed that the man shot upstairs was the Turk and this was the owner of the apartment. He confirmed that when he dug out the man's wallet and read the Italian name. The real confirmation included the man calling Jake every dirty name in the book in perfect Italian with a Naples accent.

"Listen, asshole," Jake said in English. "I understand every word. Keep talking and I'll cut off your nuts and shove them down your throat." According to the man's expression, he was also fluent in English. Good.

"Where to?" Alexandra asked in German.

"Just drive," Jake said. "This guy needs to tell us a few things."

Jake knew that actual torture worked to extract information, but often the subject would say anything to make the pain stop. Better than actually hurting someone was the fear that you would do anything up to and including kill them to make them talk. Police and certain intelligence agencies couldn't make that work, since they were constrained by things like rules and pesky laws. But Jake was an independent contractor. And as far as this man was concerned, Jake could have been with the Malavita. He used that to his advantage. So, without causing too much pain or disfigurement, Jake was able to extract everything the Italian knew about his activities.

Now the problem was what he needed to do with the guy. If Jake handed the man over to the Agency, they might actually get the same information. And he sure as hell didn't need them mucking up his operation. No. Jake would have to find another outlet. He had a few associates in Italian law enforcement, but none who could handle the leader of a potential terrorist cell. There was more going on in Rome than Jake was sure about at this time. He needed to find the next man on the rung of the ladder. That was the Italian's handler or contact. That man was in Naples.

He had a better idea. Years ago he had worked a case with an officer with the Italian External Intelligence and Security Agency. A woman named Elisa Murici. But he had no idea where she might be assigned at this time. Jake pulled out his phone and punched in the number for the officer. As the phone rang on the other end, Jake punched the Italian in the jaw, knocking him out.

Finally, a soft voice came on the phone. "I don't know this number."

It wasn't like Jake wanted to use his name, so instead he simply said in Italian, "The Stone of Archimedes was an interesting find."

"Jake?" she whispered in English. "How are you doing? By the way, your Italian has gotten quite good."

"I've been living here for a while."

"In Calabria," she said.

"You can tell?"

"Just a little. If this is what you call a booty call, I'm not in Italy."

Jake glanced to the front at Alexandra. "No, this is business." He quickly explained what he had been working on, up to the point of picking up this Italian at his apartment. "I need to drop him off with a trusted person. Anyone you trust?"

"My people are not authorized to work in Italy," Elisa explained.

"That didn't stop you last time."

"I know. And I almost got fired."

"Where are you? And why are you whispering?"

Hesitation. "Out of the country. Working a case."

"I see. Sorry to bother you. But this guy has information about a terrorist attack in Rome. Soon."

"All right. I know some people at AISI."

That would be the Italian Internal Information and Security Agency, their version of the FBI.

She gave him a location to drop off the man and said she'd call him back with a contact name.

Jake put away his phone and glanced up to Alexandra.

"Was that another old girlfriend?" she asked.

Not officially, he thought, but they had been involved in a short period of sex. Strictly sex. Before Jake could answer, he got a quick call back from Elisa telling him where to drop off the Italian. Jake thanked her and said to take care.

He told Alexandra where to go. They would make the drop in front of the Colosseum at the exit for the Metro. She turned and headed in that direction.

10

Brindisi, Italy

Elisa Murici stood at the rail of the ferry from Greece to Italy, the early-rising sun reflecting off the white buildings of this Italian coastal city. She had mixed feelings about reaching the shores of her homeland. Since her agency was established by law to only operate outside of Italy, it meant her work on this case would probably come to an end soon. She would be required to pass off this case to her colleagues with Internal Security.

But a lot had happened through the night as she crossed from Patras, Greece to Brindisi. First, she had gotten that unexpected call from Jake Adams, who had captured a suspicious man in Rome and passed him off to her counterparts with AISI. What in the hell was Jake doing in Rome? Then, in the middle of the night, she had gotten word that the captured man had not said a word to

AISI. How was that possible? What had Jake gotten from the man? She could only imagine, based on what she knew about Jake, that he had gotten anything and everything the man knew. And then an hour ago she had gotten word from her people that she would pass off the man she had tailed from Athens to an officer with AISI as soon as they reached the Italian port.

She had mostly kept her distance from the man she knew as Zamir, the potential bomb builder from Iraq. With her oversized sunglasses, she could shift her eyes without moving her head much, keeping the man in her peripheral view. She was certain she had not been burned. But once during the transit she had gotten close enough to the man to smell his overpowering aftershave, which seemed like the musk from a mink.

As the ferry closed in on the pier, those with cars were instructed over the intercom to return below deck and prepare to disembark with their vehicles. Walking passengers should make their way to the exits.

Elisa got a text and she checked her phone. It was from an unknown contact, but with the proper authorization code. It was her Internal Information and Security Agency contact. An image popped up, which she put to memory, since it disappeared within a few seconds. The photo was of a young, handsome man with long scraggly hair and tattoos on both of his forearms. He had an infectious smile that gave him the appearance of a barista and not an AISI officer. This man would be on the pier waiting for her with a car.

She followed Zamir at a distance as the ferry slowly docked at the terminal. Considering the number of passengers, this was not an easy task.

Soon, they started to disembark, and Elisa kept her eyes out for her contact and potential threats from Zamir and his people. But she guessed that if Zamir was the bomb builder, he would remain alone until he got to a contact somewhere near Rome. Somehow this Zamir had gotten a Greek passport after the Iraq War. Her people thought that the man might have been working both sides back then. Nobody knew for sure. A lot of people fell through the cracks following that conflict. The only reason Elisa had gotten involved at all was due to a number of electronic intercepts from disposable phones from Greece to Italy.

Since Italy and Greece were both part of the Schengen Agreement, customs and immigration was non-existent. They all flowed through the open border like fish through a stream.

Ahead she saw her contact wandering back and forth at the terminal exit, but obviously keeping his eyes open for both her and Zamir. When the Iraqi passed within a few feet of her contact, he didn't even acknowledge the man. The Iraqi was just another passenger.

Elisa came up to her contact, who smiled at her. They embraced like lovers and kissed each other on both cheeks.

"Vito Galati," he whispered into her ear as he continued his embrace.

She pulled back and smiled slightly. He was even more handsome than his photo, which she didn't think was possible. "Let's go. He just passed you."

"I know. Black slacks, black leather jacket. A green and black Fila bag over his left shoulder."

"Good eye," she said as she strut off.

"My car is here," Vito said.

She stopped and glanced at an old red Fiat Panda. "Budget cuts?"

"It fits in." He took her bag and threw it in the back seat, then ran around to the driver's side.

She got in to the passenger seat and buckled in. "Are you old enough to drive?"

He didn't answer.

"Well then follow that taxi before Zamir gets away," she said.

The young officer ground the gears and finally pulled out after the taxi. They wound slowly through the port area and into Brindisi.

"Do you know anything about the man they picked up in Rome last night?" she asked.

"I was not in on the interrogation," Vito said. "But I understand they got nothing from that man."

"Of course not," she said. "Your organization has certain rules and must follow them."

"We all have rules. . . What do I call you?"

"My name is Elisa. That usually works for me."

He nodded understanding. "What would you have done to extract something from this man?"

That was a damn good question, she thought. What would Jake Adams do? Anything necessary. But she couldn't let this young officer know about Jake. "I'm guessing your agency will take over from here. Where's your backup?"

Vito stared at her. Perhaps too long, considering the traffic. He turned back to his driving and said, "You have not been told?"

"Told what?"

"You have been authorized special authority to work on assignment with AISI," he said.

Part of her wanted nothing less than that. But now she too would be forced to comply with certain rules. "All right," she said.

"I guess you could say you work for me," Vito said with a smile.

"You can say anything you want," she said. "But if you ever say that again, I'll neuter you. Capisco?"

Vito swallowed hard. "Si."

"Don't follow so close," she instructed.

"Were you able to get a tracking device on him?" he asked.

She laughed under her breath. "What do you think? The man is not an idiot. I could not get within five meters of the man." This was a lie.

"What about his phone?"

"He uses a disposable. And my guess is that one is somewhere on the bottom of the Adriatic."

"I understand. Where do you think he's going?"

"Central train station," she surmised.

"Not the airport?"

She shook her head. "This guy likes to work with cash. You can still buy a train ticket with Euros."

"Makes sense. Especially now."

By this time they had traveled from the east side where the port sat to the central train station, which was a small sepia structure with multiple arched windows trimmed in white.

Zamir got out of his taxi and hurried into the train station.

"Hurry up and park this tin can," Elisa said. "Just pull over and let me out. You can catch up to me."

She got out and grabbed her bag from the back seat. Then she stepped swiftly toward the front entrance. If this man was in a hurry, then he must have been trying to catch a train that would leave soon.

Once she got inside, she saw her target walk away from the ticket booth and move toward the outer platforms. Another man had gotten to the ticket window first, but Elisa pushed the man aside and leaned into the window, asking for the destination of the last man.

"Roma," the ticket agent said.

Elisa bought two tickets for the same train.

"It leaves in just a few minutes," the agent said. "Platform Two."

"Sorry," she said to the man she had pushed. Then she hurried toward the platform just as Vito came rushing into the front door.

He caught up with her and now the two of them simply looked like a couple in a hurry to catch their train. They barely made it on the train before it slowly pulled away from the central train station.

They settled into a set of chairs facing forward, discussing openly how close they had cut it. She had no idea where Zamir was on the train, but she guessed she had a while to find him. The problem was, she would need to try to do something to change her appearance. This man wasn't a moron. She had been on him in Athens, but from a longer distance. Then she had followed him to the ferry in Patras, had crossed the Adriatic with him, and now they were on the same train from Brindisi to Rome. Coincidences happened. But this was more than kismet.

11

Zurich, Switzerland

Derrick Konrad had traveled on the night train from Geneva following the man who had escaped their raid near the airport. He had no idea where this man was going, but he just knew that the man had to be aware of the raid and this guy was escaping. Konrad had two choices now. He could simply arrest the man and link him to the others, or he could follow him and hopefully lead him to someone higher up the food chain. Deep down, he had a feeling this man was preparing to strike in Switzerland—probably somewhere in the financial district of Zurich, where the strength of the country's banks were headquartered. Here they could strike a blow to the rich and famous of the world. The one percent.

After the long train ride, his suspect had wandered in the early morning hours to a coffee shop across from the Zurich Hauptbahnhof, the main train station.

Holgar, his colleague from the Swiss Polizei, had gone to his apartment in Geneva, packed some clothes in a duffle bag, and flown to Zurich on a Polizei jet, getting there hours prior to his train arrival. The most important thing his colleague had picked up for him was his Carbamazepine to prevent seizures. He was down to just one pill on him, not thinking he would be leaving Geneva without warning. His epilepsy was controlled for now, but he never knew when a seizure would strike.

While his Polizei friend kept an eye on the suspect, he quickly got into the back seat of his friend's car and changed his shirt after applying a heavy dose of underarm deodorant.

"Is our scumbag still drinking coffee?" Konrad asked.

"Yes, sir. His second dose."

"Could you hand me the water?"

His associate kept his eyes on the café while he reached back with the bottle of water. Then he took a quick glance back as Konrad took his medication. Only a few people knew about his affliction, and that's the way he wanted it to stay. He had discussed his epilepsy with Holgar one night while they staked out the three men in Geneva. Part of his involvement with INTERPOL was due to the fact that it was difficult for him to have a partner. Once they found out he might end up on the ground flopping like a fish during an important moment, nobody trusted him. But Holgar didn't seem too concerned.

"When was your last. . .incident?" Holgar asked.

"Two years, three months and four days," Konrad said.

"How do you drive?"

"Very carefully." He hesitated and then said, "I've learned to identify when a seizure might be coming on. So I pull over. I've had a lot of false alarms, but that's better than the alternative."

Holgar nodded his head in agreement.

Konrad zipped up his bag and went back to the front passenger seat. He glanced at his partner, who seemed a bit distracted. "You see, this is why I don't tell people about my little demon. It changes our relationship."

"I'm sorry, Derrick. I'm just tired. Seriously, it doesn't matter to me."

"But we must be there at all times for our partners," Konrad said. "And I can't give you one hundred percent certainty of that."

"I'll take your experience any day. You have a great reputation. You get the bad guys. That's all that matters to me."

"Thank you." Konrad shifted his head toward the café. "What do you think he's doing?"

Holgar shrugged. "Waiting for a contact?"

"Not likely." He pointed behind him, across the street at the Hauptbahnhof. "Why stay here?"

"He doesn't have a friend or associate to bring him a bag of clothes," Holgar said with a smirk.

"That's right. He left in a hurry without any baggage. But why stay here?"

Holgar looked confused.

Konrad filled in the blanks. "The coffee shop in the train station wasn't open yet. It doesn't open for another half hour. So, this guy is waiting for another train."

"To where?" Holgar asked.

"That is the question of the morning, Holgar." He raised a finger as he found his phone. Then he quickly called a number from memory and waited. His contact in the Swiss Federal Office of Police finally answered and asked how things were going. Just great. He briefed the boss on their current situation, speculating on how the suspect might be catching another train. He made a crass joke about throwing the man off somewhere once the train got up to speed. Then Konrad asked the important question. When he did so, Holgar looked surprised. But the boss agreed with Konrad.

He got off the phone and shoved it back in his pocket.

"What did he say?" Holgar asked.

"He said you can work with me as long as I need you. Are you ready for a little adventure, Holgar?"

"Hell yes."

"All right. Here's the plan." He detailed how they would layer their surveillance of this man. As far as Konrad knew, their suspect had no idea he was being followed. That would be their advantage. And he was determined to get to the bottom of this. Whatever this was.

12

Naples, Italy

Jake always thought that Rome was the heart of Italy. Naples, or Napoli to the Italians, was the rectum with leaky oily discharge. Garbage lay strewn everywhere, graffiti a ubiquitous display by would-be artists with too much colorful paint and no real jobs to distract from their real passion. Which was a shame, Jake thought. With the location on the sea and Mt. Vesuvius for a backdrop, Naples could have been the most beautiful city in Italy. Instead, it was like a morbidly obese man with smelly cheese lurking in the fat folds. But Naples also had the best pizza in the world, so there was that.

He had worked in Naples during his time in the CIA, thwarting a bombing in the 80s with his new friend Toni Contardo. At the time he didn't realize the significance of that new relationship, or that it would develop into a love affair and friendship that would result in the birth of his first child, Karl. In the past fifteen hours he kept seeing glimpses of Toni, with her long curly black hair, until he realized the woman was not her and he felt like a total idiot, shaking his head as if wiping clear an etch-a-sketch. Of course, he didn't mention this to his current girlfriend, Alexandra. But he sensed that she knew something wasn't quite right with him.

The two of them had tried to track down the man that the Italian in Rome had given up after considerable persuasion. The guy wasn't at his apartment. He had no traditional work, so they couldn't track him down there. They had no choice but to wait out the man at his favorite pizza place across the street from his apartment.

It was late afternoon now and Jake had just finished one of those famous Napoli pizzas. He worked on his second Peroni beer, his back against the corner booth with a view of the front door and a back exit.

"Do you think that asshole in Rome gave us bad information?" Alexandra asked. She still had a couple of pieces of pizza left, and was nursing her first beer.

"I don't think so," Jake said. "I can tell when someone is lying to me." But she knew that.

Jake had been able to get a passport photo of the man from his Agency contacts, but that was at least five years old. The guy could have changed his appearance by now.

"Have you heard anything from Russo?" she asked.

"You know he doesn't have my cell number," Jake said. Only a few people in the world had that.

"You protect your number like nuclear codes."

His cell phone was probably more secure than nuclear codes. Every text going in or out was highly encrypted. Calls were run through multiple servers and could not be traced by even the NSA, the CIA, or the FBI. The GPS was deflected to various locations around the world. It currently had him somewhere in Peru.

"Just trying to stay one step ahead of the hackers. Or the internet marketers. Here we go. Coming through the door. That's our guy."

The man had not changed much from his passport photo. He even had the skinny beard and the black eye liner. Put a sail on the man and he would end up on Vesuvius in a stiff breeze.

They had discussed how they wanted to play the guy. Luckily the man in Rome had given them some inside information about the man's desires. Pizza was one. Tall blonde women were another. That's where Alexandra came to play. She pulled out her map of Naples and strut to the bar, pretending to be totally lost.

From Jake's angle, he could see Alexandra turned away from the man, who was more than a little interested. He couldn't keep his eyes off of her nice butt. She flicked her hair seductively and ran a finger across the map.

The subject couldn't handle it. He got up from his chair and approached Alexandra. Jake couldn't hear what he was saying, but he could see their expressions. She was damn good and the subject was being reeling in like a fish. Once the man nuzzled closer and pointed out something on the map, Jake knew they had him. Especially after Alexandra whispered something in the man's ear, smiled, and turned, swaying her hips toward the bathroom. The guy looked around and then followed her.

Jake paid and headed out the back door to the alley. When he got outside, he noticed two things. First, darkness had almost set in. And second, Alexandra had their subject in a sleeper hold and he was struggling for air like that fish on the line. In a few seconds the man passed out in Alexandra's arms. Jake patted the guy down, finding a gun and a switchblade.

"Did you at least let him touch your boobs?" Jake asked.

She shrugged. "He tried."

They had parked their car in the back lot, so she dragged the thin man to the trunk, and the two of them threw him in roughly and quietly closed the trunk door on him.

Then they drove to an isolated location down by the commercial shipping docks. They had scoped out the location earlier in the day and guessed it would be a great place to interrogate someone.

Lights from the city glistened off the sea, giving tourists in the city a false sense of security. But Jake knew that darkness in Naples brought out every dirtbag from the underworld—from petty street criminals to those heavy hitters in organized crime. It was the most dangerous city in Italy and rivaled in the Mediterranean only by those in the south regions of North Africa and the Middle East.

When he stopped he saw that Alexandra was messing with her phone. "Are you checking on Emma?" he asked her.

"No. This is Russo. He said the Italians finally came and picked up Marisa at the hotel a couple of hours ago. He's on the north end of Naples."

Jake wasn't entirely sure he wanted to continue working with a man from the Mafia. But he had to admit that the man knew Italy much better than Jake, and he had a lot of contacts in Naples. "Did you send him this way?"

"Do you want me to?"

"Yeah. He might come in handy with the man in the trunk. He can name drop and let the guy know we aren't with the authorities. It might speed up our work."

The guy was still passed out in the trunk, curled up like a baby. Jake pulled the man out by himself, hoisting him over his shoulder with ease. Alexandra opened an old metal container that was probably no longer in use and had been used recently to store folded boxes awaiting recycling. The boxes filled the back end of the container, leaving them the front half.

Jake tried to set the man down gently on the metal surface, but he lost his grip and the man's head bounced off the hard surface, waking him up. But now the guy was groggy and holding his head.

Alexandra pulled out a set of heavy zip ties and bound the man's hands behind his back. Then she strapped his skinny ankles with another one.

"That's good," Jake said in German. "He isn't going anywhere."

She pulled out some other items they had purchased earlier in the day. They would first start with the soft approach. Then Jake would discover what the man feared most to exploit that as best he could. Most people feared basic elements—water and fire. But they also liked to keep various items, like teeth and fingers and balls and penile tissue.

First, they made sure to wake the man up and lit the container with a small portable light. Then Jake started to work up a sequence with various tools of destruction, from the man's own switchblade to simple pliers. They also had a number of bottles of water and a butane torch. The man's eyes got wider as Jake played with each item.

Alexandra got a call from Russo before they got started with their interrogation. She told him how to find them.

Moments later, Russo came into the container and gave a little whistle. In English he said, "Are you sure you don't want to work for me?"

"You can't afford us," Jake said. "You want to start this with a few questions? It might save with the pain and disbursal of DNA."

Russo pulled Jake out of earshot of the man. "How do you want to play this?"

"Play up your association with the Calabrese Malavita," Jake said. "I'm guessing you can drop a few names that will scare the shit out of him."

"Got it," Russo said. Then he went to the man and lifted him off the ground by his shirt, setting him on his butt. He slapped him across the face about ten times before saying a word. Then he went into a quick diatribe with the man, which made it difficult for Jake to keep up. His Italian was good, but this was something else—like a father bitch-slapping a son to find out why he was tormenting his sister. Finally, Russo mentioned a couple of names, making the man's eyes widen with fear.

Their subject started to cry like a little girl, tears streaking his face and snot rolling from his nostrils. Now Jake held Russo back and let the subject wallow for a moment. Alexandra found the rag they planned on using to water board the man, and she wiped the tears and snot from the man's face.

In the end, it took just a few calm words from Russo to make the man talk. It turned out that family was very important to guys like Russo. When a lower-level thug is forced to realize the importance of keeping friends and relatives safe, the choice becomes quite clear. Talk or see the complete elimination of familial DNA from this Earth.

Jake and Russo stepped outside while Alexandra kept watch over the man.

"You think that's all the man knows?" Russo asked.

"I think so." And that was a problem. Someone had set up a highly compartmentalized organization.

"What do we do with this guy?"

"We need to stash him for a while," Jake said. "At least until we can find his contact in Pompeii tomorrow."

"There are cameras everywhere in Pompeii."

"I know. But we don't have a choice. That's where the meeting is set up. He has no other way to contact the next man up the chain."

Russo put his hand on Jake's shoulder. "Don't worry. My people run most of the historic sites in this region. We have people who can shut down the cameras tomorrow."

Jake knew the Malavita was connected, but he had no idea just how much. "All right. Can you babysit this guy until after the meeting?"

"I know a guy and a place," Russo said.

That was becoming a theme for his Mafia friend.

"On the other hand, I also know a guy with a fishing boat." Russo gave Jake a broad smile.

"I understand. But I might need the guy for another kind of bait down the road."

"All right. We'll sit on him for now."

Jake opened the container door and waved for Alexandra. She had gathered all of the gear into the bag, so she slung that over her shoulder and came out.

"We might need this stuff," she said.

The two of them headed back to the car. Now they needed to find a place to stay for the night.

13

Rome, Italy

Elisa Murici had traveled most of the day with her new friend from AISI, Vito Galati, by train from Brindisi to Rome. It had not taken much to keep track of Zamir at first. The man had gotten a cheap ticket in the second-class car. She and Vito had taken turns moving from their first-class car to the second class one, where budget-minded folks where jammed together like an airline.

There was no great route to travel from the southeast coastal city of Brindisi to the capital city of Rome. Their ticket routed them along the coast to Bari, where they took on new passengers and perhaps dropped off a few. The train headed north for a while before cutting across the Apennines toward Rome. It was a beautiful ride, but Elisa had a lot on her mind. Officially she had nothing on this man named Zamir. For all she knew the man could have been going to Rome to visit old friends or to see the ancient sites.

Her opinion changed about an hour after leaving the coastal city of Bari. Zamir was missing. Sure, he could have been wandering the train with restless legs. Many people couldn't sit still very long. But then she had gone to one end of the train and her colleague had gone to the other end. Together, along with two porters, they had swept toward the middle, making sure to check every bathroom. Nothing. The man had disappeared.

There was only one conclusion. Zamir had somehow gotten off the train in Bari. But why? Did he know they were following him? She was sure she had not been burned, but she could not yet trust her young associate. What skills did he possess?

They had pulled into Rome a couple of hours ago and both of their bosses were not happy. Elisa wasn't used to failing at such an epic level. She had to redeem herself. But how?

Then she thought about the phone call she had gotten from Jake Adams. Jake had rounded up a man who he suspected was part of a terrorist cell plotting something against Rome. That man had been turned over to the Internal Information and Security Agency, Vito's organization. AISI had the man on ice, but they were not getting much out of him.

Elisa took a pass at the man, but he didn't seem to be overly forthcoming. As an Italian citizen, the man knew his rights and the fact that they could not beat him for the information. And then the truth and realization fell onto her chest like a truckload of stones. Why had Jake Adams turned over this man to AISI? There was only one reason to do so—Jake had gotten everything he needed from this man, and he had turned him over for potential prosecution. But that was against Jake's nature. He would be more prone to extracting data and then make sure the man couldn't do anymore harm. Jake wasn't a take prisoner kind of guy. He had once said that evil existed in the hearts of some men, and love could not change their hearts. The only thing those people understood was strength. A bullet to the head, Jake had intimated.

Now she stood in the darkness outside of the AISI headquarters building, her colleague Vito sitting in his agency car a block away waiting for her.

She reluctantly pulled out her cell phone and punched in the number that had called her when she was on the ferry.

"How's my favorite Italian?" Jake Adams asked.

"I'm in Rome," she said. "Is there any way we can get together tonight?"

Hesitation on the other end. Finally, Jake said, "Is this a booty call?"

"Ha, ha. It was a legitimate question, considering our past." She turned and glanced at her colleague, and then swiveled around so he couldn't read her lips. "I just talked with our Italian friend. The one you scared shitless. The one who refuses to say a damn thing to us."

Jake said nothing.

She continued, "What did you get from him?"

Letting out a slight sigh, Jake said, "You know I can't tell you that."

"You no longer work for the CIA," she reminded him.

"Thank God."

"Then why not help a girl out?"

"No offense. But I don't know those at Internal."

"You know me."

"True. I'm guessing they assigned someone to babysit you in Italy, otherwise you wouldn't still be working the case."

"Please, Jake."

"You sound desperate."

She twisted her head again for a second to look at Vito. Then she exhaled and said, "I screwed up."

"How?"

Reluctantly, she told him about the potential Iraqi bomb builder she had been watching in Athens. How she had followed him on the ferry to Brindisi. And then the tough part—how she had lost the man on the train, perhaps in Bari.

"It happens," Jake said. "The man bought a ticket to Rome?"

"That's what the ticket agent said."

"I've done similar things in the past," he said. "He probably got off in Bari and waited to pick up the next train to Rome. Or, he could have bought a ticket to somewhere else. He could be anywhere in Italy now."

She knew that, and that's why she was beating herself up so much. "I know. What do I do now?" She hoped he would take pity on her and divulge what the man had told him.

"Do you know of any ties the Iraqi has in Rome?"

"No. We know very little about the man. We do know that he worked both sides during the Iraq War. He was giving up intel while building IEDs for the bad guys."

"Then why in the hell did they let the guy live?" Jake asked.

"Good question. That's above my level, though. But now we have what we have. What did you discover from this man you picked up in Rome?"

Pause. Jake finally said, "He didn't know much. He simply called his group the eyes."

"They were a scouting team."

"I believe so," he confirmed.

"What are the targets?"

"The usual suspects, I would guess," Jake said. "Nearly every major tourist attraction in Rome, religious and otherwise."

"But those have been hardened," she assured him.

"Not enough. We had a shootout with a couple of his team."

"The two men you killed."

"In self defense."

"Right. And then the third one at the man's apartment."

"I didn't kill him."

"Someone did. A friend of yours?"

"Something like that. Anyway, that's how we got the man you're talking with."

"That's all the man told you? That they were the eyes?"

"As you know, that's the most important part of a terrorist plot—good intelligence. And I'm telling you that Rome has flaws with their security profile. You're vulnerable."

She knew this. Although that wasn't technically her job, she could give recommendations.

"What do you want from me?" Jake asked.

"Anything you can give me. If the cell you broke up was the eyes, then I might have just lost part of the brain. The bomb maker. We must find him. Was I not helpful last time?"

"Yes, you were." Jake paused, obviously thinking. "Your Italian friend gave us the name of his contact."

"What? Why are you just telling me this now?"

"The last time we talked," Jake said, "it wasn't like you were overly forthcoming."

"I was undercover in close proximity to my target. I shouldn't have been on the phone at all. Maybe that's how the Iraqi burned me."

"I doubt it. The Iraqi was probably simply following a pre-determined route to avoid detection. It happens."

"What's the contact's name," she demanded.

Jake grunted.

"Come on. I need your help."

Reluctantly, Jake gave up the man's name and location.

"So, Napoli. I'm guessing you're there now."

"Not exactly."

"You've already found the man."

Jake said nothing. Then he gave her the address of the contact in Napoli.

"Thanks, Jake."

"Not a problem. But are you even sure the Iraqi is related to the man you have in custody?"

"We have nothing else to go on."

"Be careful," he said. "These people are dangerous."

But not as dangerous as Jake Adams, she guessed. They cut their call off and she wandered back to the car. She got in and tapped the GPS.

"Did you get something?" Vito asked her.

"A lead in Napoli."

"Are we going there in the morning?"

"No. We're going there right now." She had a feeling Jake might be telling her the truth, but not the whole truth. He wouldn't have given up the man's name and location if he hadn't already found the guy. Yet, she had no other options.

"Can I stop by my apartment to get a few items?" Vito asked.

"Yes. I'll do the same. My clothes from my trip are all dirty."

"My place is only two kilometers from here."

She waved her left hand while she continued to put in the address of the man Jake had given her from Napoli. Deep down she had a feeling that time was not a real issue this evening.

•

Jake stood naked in his hotel room, having just gotten off the phone with Elisa Murici. He hated lying to her. She had been a great asset to him in the past, and that had nothing to do with the sexual encounters they had experienced. He peered around the curtain at the lights of Naples in the distance. Technically he was in the city of Pompeii, so he had not lied to Elisa.

"Jake, would you get that nice ass of yours back to bed?" Alexandra said.

They had made love earlier and he wondered now if she was ready for round two. Or perhaps she was just a bit chilled by the cool room.

He set his phone on the nightstand and slid under the sheets. She nuzzled next to him and grasped onto his partial erection.

"Was that your old girlfriend again?" she asked.

Jake had no intention of answering that. Instead, fully erect now, he flipped her over and took her from behind. Hard and fast. But he felt guilty for doing so, since he was thinking about Elisa while he was pounding Alexandra.

14

Innsbruck, Austria

Derrick Konrad had been correct, the man he had followed from Geneva to Zurich had gotten off the train in the capital city and simply waited for his next train to Innsbruck, Austria. Konrad had gotten on the train with his Swiss Polizei colleague, Holgar, and watched the man from a distance. He had even called his boss at INTERPOL when the train crossed into Austria, trying to simply pull the man in for interrogation. The problem was tying the man to the bomb making equipment at the apartment in the western suburb of Vernier, near the Geneva Airport. The Swiss Polizei had to get something from the two men captured in that raid. They had all three on voice recording, but there had been no real smoking gun with what they had discussed there. Perhaps his boss was right telling Konrad to stick with the bomb maker. Now, with the entry to Austria, they had a problem. Holgar was a Swiss Polizei officer with no authority to act in Austria. Konrad had asked for authorization to assign Holgar officially, at least on a temporary assignment, with INTERPOL. That would give Holgar authority to act worldwide, with some restrictions, and within the European Union countries with near impunity.

Now, the train slowly pulled out of the Innsbruck Hauptbahnhof. They were all on the night train from Innsbruck to Venice, Italy. The dirtbag potential terrorist was in a car with a row of seats on both sides facing each other. A fairly plush car. But Konrad and Holgar had been able to get a private sleeper car, which they had already converted from seats to beds.

Konrad stood and glanced out the window at the city lights. He had been on this train before, but that had been in the winter during the ski season. Now the trees were mostly bare awaiting the snow. Already a chill was in the air. He could tell that at the main train station in Innsbruck. Warm lights reflected off the colorful buildings along the swift-flowing Inn River that cut through the city.

"Derrick, I just got a text from our headquarters. I am authorized to work with you under the INTERPOL umbrella."

Checking out his partner's reflection in the window, Konrad nodded his head. "That's good." It wasn't like they would have said no. For the Swiss Polizei that was a win-win situation. If Konrad and Holgar screwed up, the Polizei could blame it on INTERPOL. If they succeeded in bringing down a terrorist network, the Swiss could claim that it was a joint operation between the Polizei and INTERPOL. And both Holgar and Konrad were officially Swiss citizens. But Konrad didn't care about recognition. He only cared about results.

Turning back to his partner, Konrad said, "Where do you think this man is going?"

Holgar shrugged and placed his hands on his hips. "Venice."

"For now, yes. But I mean in the end. What's his plan?"

"I've been thinking about that since leaving Zurich," Holgar said. "I thought the plan was to strike somewhere in the banking district of the city. But now I don't know."

Konrad was equally confused. Why work with those other men in Geneva only to depart in a hurry? Finally, he said, "The man's plans had to change after we raided the apartment."

"Makes sense." Holgar seemed to be in deep thought as he grasped onto the ladder leading to the top bunk. He asked, "Did your boss mention what they got from those men at the apartment?"

"Nothing new," Konrad said. "I thought they would give us something. Anything."

"Maybe they don't know much."

"They know more than they're saying," Konrad assured his young associate. "Sometimes I wish we could take the gloves off and pound some sense into these criminals."

"You mean terrorists."

"Terrorist criminals. That's the problem, you see. We treat them as if they plan to rob a bank. But really they want to change our way of life. They come to our country because we allow them in. Then they try to change us into something we are not. And we can't allow that, Holgar. We must fight them with every cell in our bodies. They can't survive. They are a malignant tumor that must be sliced out."

"The only good terrorist is a dead terrorist," Holgar said with a smirk.

"Something like that." Exactly like that, he thought. "But sometimes we must follow the ant back to the colony and kill them all. Otherwise we just get the scout and more will follow. We must douse the entire ant hill with petro and light it on fire. Kill them all before they kill us."

Konrad sat on the lower bunk and dropped onto his back, his eyes closed. This was the only way they could succeed, he thought. This scout would lead them to the colony.

15

Pompeii, Italy

For the first time in weeks, Jake had actually allowed himself to sleep in past 0600. Since the site of the ruins at Pompeii didn't open until 0830, they had time for a leisurely breakfast and plenty of coffee. Their meeting was scheduled for 0900 in a remote corner of the ruins. Jake had found a map of the complex and plotted out a strategy. He was depending on Russo to control the security feeds to that area. Alexandra would back him up by making sure the contact had no escape. But Jake knew that this place was massive, having been there a couple of times.

He and Alexandra got to the ruins at the opening, making sure to get in to position early. Since Jake had no photo of his contact, he was depending on the contact carrying a telescoping rod with a baby blue flag on top—the type used by tour guides to keep tourists lined up like cattle.

Jake wandered around pretending to take photos with his phone. While he did so, he made sure to find all of the cameras scattered among the ruins. But there was no way to find them all, he thought.

"In position," Jake said into his mic.

"Auch," Alexandra said.

Glancing about the area, Jake didn't like what he saw. There were two ways into the location. The first way went back toward the front entrance, and the second way rounded the outer edge of the ruins toward the coliseum, a smaller version of Rome's main attraction. But Jake had a plan for both options, if it should come to that. Alexandra was in position to handle the back escape, and Jake would handle the short way. If the contact got past the both of them, Russo would be waiting at the exit. The problem was Russo would have to be contacted by cell phone. He wasn't wearing a comm unit.

Jake could see why the contact wanted to meet here, though. It was perhaps the most isolated location in the vast ruins. Other places highlighted elaborate villas with mosaic tiles and beautiful terraces. Others showed macabre scenes of human remains curled up as death came to them, covering them with feet of pumice and ash. Here, though, was a long passageway that probably served back in the day as an outer wall road used by security.

A couple of minutes after 0900, a group of some 15 tourists wandered through the area. They appeared to be older folks from Germany. The tour guide was a man in his early 40s with dark hair and a full beard. He was speaking German with an Italian accent. More importantly, he held a telescoping rod with a light blue flag on top. The tour guide instructed his people to continue down the road and take a right at the end. They could take a bathroom break down there and he would catch up with them.

Jake didn't make a move toward the tour guide until the tourists were well down the stone road.

Meanwhile, the tour guide had his phone out and was checking something, or pretending to do so. His eyes kept on gazing at Jake, who was trying his best to remain indifferent.

Finally, once the tourists had rounded the corner and were out of sight, Jake drifted over to the tour guide and gave the man the code phrase he had gotten from the Italian in Naples the night before.

The tour guide was suddenly on high alert. "I don't understand," he said in Italian.

"Our friend in Naples could not make it today," Jake explained. "He is a little tied up."

The man's eyes shifted like a rat trying to escape from a cat. Then he ran.

"Damn it," Jake said aloud. "He's running your way."

Jake pulled his gun and went after the man. Suddenly, he could see Alexandra step around the corner ahead, her gun out and at the side of her leg. The man stopped in his tracks and turned into a structure.

Both Jake and Alexandra got to the entrance at the same time. "I don't think there's a way out," Jake said. "Wait here."

Inside, with the sun not up all the way, the structure was dark and gloomy. It was a larger villa, Jake guessed, with an inner solarium and terrace, the floors a patchwork of mosaic tiles that appeared to be under reconstruction.

The first shot came and startled Jake slightly, the bullet striking a wall next to him. It came from up the stairs, so Jake continued forward. He really needed to take this man alive.

"Are you all right, Jake?" came Alexandra's voice in his ear piece.

"Fine. Moving forward," he answered.

He could see a set of stairs ahead. Before going up the stairs, which would leave him vulnerable, Jake said, "I just want to talk to you."

The Italian called him a fucking liar. Harsh.

With his gun aimed up the stairway, Jake kept his body against the right wall and stepped lightly upward as quietly as possible. When he saw movement at the top left, Jake tried to hold back from pulling the trigger. But the man shot twice in his direction. Jake returned fire with one round, shooting low.

Then nothing. Jake could hear his own heart pounding in his chest. Keep him alive, he kept telling himself.

"Come on," Jake said. "I don't want to hurt you."

The Italian said some shit about contorting the body in an unnatural way. If men could do that, they wouldn't need women.

He took a couple more steps upward.

The man rounded the corner again. But Jake was ready for him. Before the man could fire, Jake shot once, hitting the man in the leg and dropping him to the hard surface.

Jake rushed up the stairs and stepped on the man's right hand, trapping the gun against the ground. Then he pulled the gun out of the guy's hand and looked at the man who was holding his left leg, blood pouring out of the wound. Damn it.

"Get up here," Jake said into his mic. Then he stooped down next to the injured man. "This is bad. You need to give me your contact."

The man grit his teeth in pain. "Fuck you."

Alexandra ran up and looked down at the man. "Damn."

"Yeah, I'm pretty sure I hit the femoral artery," Jake said. "He has less than ten minutes to live."

The injured man's eyes widened.

"Let's just leave him," Alexandra said in German. "We need to get out now. Everybody had to have heard those shots."

"No," Jake said, switching to English. "This guy's going to give us his contact."

"You are not Italian," the man said, his eyes starting to swirl. "Not Italian Polizia? Carabinieri?"

"Hell no," Jake said. "We're independent contractors."

"You must call an ambulance," the Italian said.

"I must do nothing," Jake said. "You're a dirtbag terrorist. I should put a bullet in your head."

"No, no. I am a simple anarchist."

"Right. And I'm Santa Claus."

"It's true." The man looked close to passing out.

"All right. Then who do you work for?"

"I am just a messenger."

"The man from Naples reported to you and you gave him instructions," Jake said. "That's pretty organized for an anarchist." He stopped for a reaction, but the guy was drifting farther from this world. "Who do you report to?"

The man bit his lower lip. Finally, he muttered, "Royal Positano. Bartender."

"What's his name?"

"I don't know her name."

Okay. A female bartender at a hotel in Positano. That was something.

"Can we save him?" she asked.

Jake pulled Alexandra aside and whispered to her, "Not a chance. He has a minute or two." He handed the man's gun to her and then went back to the man, rifling through the guy's pockets to pull all identification. He needed to make it look like a simple robbery. He even found the man's blue flag and ripped that from the telescoping rod.

"Kill me," the man mumbled.

Jake didn't respond. He simply hurried down the stairs and back out to the old stone street. Alexandra came to Jake's side and held his arm like the lover she was to him. Together they wandered back out through the ruins toward the exit. They both fully expected the Polizia to be rushing toward the shots fired, but that never happened. The walls were thick and the remote location must have saved them.

As they walked out through the ruins, they met up with Russo.

"Everything all right?" Russo asked.

"Just great," Jake said. "What say we go to the Amalfi Coast?"

Russo looked up to the sky. "It looks like it will be a nice sunny day on the Amalfi."

"Did you cut all the camera feeds?" she asked.

Hesitating a second, Russo finally said, "Of course."

16

Naples, Italy

Elisa Murici and her colleague, Vito Galati, had gotten to the address she had gotten from Jake Adams sometime in the middle of the night. They had simply watched for a while from the street before finally going in to see what they could find. The two of them spent more than an hour sifting through every piece of paper in the apartment.

Meanwhile, Vito had called in to his organization for any information they could find on the man. But the guy had almost nothing on him. A few petty street crimes and protests, resulting in a couple of nights in the local jail to cool down. The guy had no social media profile. Maybe some of these turds were finally starting to get smart, Elisa thought.

Finding nothing of significance, the two of them went to a hotel and got a little rest. Luckily, they were able to find a room with two beds.

They slept in, having been up most of the night. Then, around eight in the morning, Vito's phone suddenly rang.

He picked up and listened carefully. Then he thanked the caller and set his phone back down on the end table.

"Something important?" she asked.

Vito sat up in bed but kept his lower body covered. She couldn't help but stare at his hairy muscled chest. The guy was ripped, she thought.

"Do you have a problem?" she asked.

He pushed down on his crotch. "Sometimes in the morning."

She turned her head and pointed toward the bathroom. "Better take a leak."

Vito got up and went to the bathroom and she couldn't help taking a glance at his butt as he left. Very solid.

Moments later and Vito came back, his erection reduced but still prominent in his boxer briefs.

"Put some pants on," she said. "And a shirt."

"Sorry," he said. "I normally sleep naked."

"Not in my room you don't. What did the caller say?"

"We have to get going," he said. "The local Polizia found a man wandering the streets down by the port a couple hours ago. He gave them a story of a man and woman kidnapping him and bringing him to a container to torture him for information."

"What kind of torture?"

Vito swished his head. "He said it never came to that. A third person came and threatened to do unspeakable things to him and his entire family."

Her mind went directly to Jake Adams. "Why would he divulge this information freely?"

"Because he fears the Polizia much less than those three people who took him. He wants protection."

"What did he tell them?"

"Nothing more. He said he wouldn't talk with anyone but you."

"Me? Are you sure?"

"He gave the Polizia your name, but not your organization. When they did a search, your name was coded as an intelligence asset. They contacted your agency, and they simply gave them my number."

This scenario had Jake Adams written all over it. Jake had put the fear of God in this man and then made sure he became a bread crumb to follow.

They checked out of the hotel after getting a quick cappuccino, and then drove down to the Naples Polizia station holding the man.

Elisa went in to the interrogation room alone with the man. He was nervous, no doubt, squirming in his seat like a snake with a predator nearby.

"What time is it?" the man asked Elisa.

"Why does that matter? You will spend a lot of time in prison, where time doesn't matter."

The man scratched his head and let out a deep breath. "Please," he said. "I must know the time."

She glanced at her wristwatch and guessed it didn't matter to give him that one bit of information. Perhaps it would make him more open to talk with her. Speed things up. "It's a few minutes until nine," Elisa said.

The man smiled and nodded his head. "All right. What would you like to know?"

"Everything."

"I don't know everything."

"Everything you know, then."

The man said, "I must have protection."

"From the men who took you?"

"It was two men and a woman. One man and a woman were not native Italian speakers. The woman had a German accent."

"And the other man?"

"He was Italian."

"Which man threatened you?" she asked. Not that it mattered.

"The Italian."

Now that was surprising. She would have expected Jake to do that. "Are you sure?"

"Of course. I was more afraid of the other man. He looked like he would snap my neck for farting. But he let the Italian warn me."

She waited for the man to explain.

"The Italian mentioned a few names known in the region. Names which I can no longer remember. You understand. Anyway, this man was Malavita."

Jake was working with a Mafia member. That was strange, she thought. "Are you sure?"

He nodded his head vehemently.

"And what did you tell them?" she needed to know.

Their discussion went like that for another fifteen minutes, with Elisa asking for the simple truth and the man deflecting.

"What time is it now?" the man asked.

She looked at her watch and said, "Almost quarter after nine. Why?"

"I can tell you now because it doesn't matter."

The man told her about the meeting he was supposed to have with his contact. The meeting that Jake and his friends would take in his place.

Elisa got up quickly and rushed out of the room. She instructed the Polizia to hold the man until someone from Vito's organization could pick the guy up. Then she and Vito hurried out of the building.

Once in the car, Vito behind the wheel, he asked her, "Do you think the man is telling you the truth?"

"Yes. Hurry up. Drive to Pompeii."

By the time they drove the short distance to the Pompeii ruins entrance, Elisa knew that they were too late, which is why the man she questioned was so concerned about the time. Polizia cars lined the street leading to the front gate and an ambulance sat near the turnstiles.

They parked and Vito flashed his AISI credentials to the on-scene commander. "What happened?" Vito asked.

"A shooting."

Elisa glanced over and saw a group of tourists huddled together. She wandered over and listened to their conversations. Then she used her German to ask what they knew. Some heard shots. Others thought it was fireworks. How many shots? Five. Ten. Mixed reports. But when their tour guide didn't meet up with them, they got concerned and a few of the men went to look for him. They found the man dead in one of the nearby villas. Since they had just met the tour guide, they didn't know much about the man. He was Italian, but the tour was given in English.

Moments later a small electric cart rolled down the hill toward the front gate carrying a couple of ambulance workers and a body strapped to the back end covered by a black sheet. She knew that the ruins would do everything in their power to get rid of the Polizia cars and the ambulance. Then they would spread the word that a tourist had experienced a heart attack. Nothing to see here.

Elisa and Vito went to the cart carrying the dead man, and she insisted on looking at the man.

"Any identification?" she asked the EMTs.

"No, ma'am. Not even a cell phone."

"Where was he shot?" Vito asked.

"In the leg. But the bullet obviously tore through his femoral artery. He never had a chance."

A leg wound, Elisa thought. That meant that Jake and friends wanted to get information from this man, not kill him. But the shot had been too good nonetheless.

Realizing they would get nothing more from the body, Elisa went back to the on-scene Polizia commander and asked about surveillance cameras. There were many throughout the ruins, the man said. But for some reason they were not working.

The Polizia man turned to a young man standing with another officer. "But this boy got a video of two people leaving the ruins. It might be important."

Vito took the lead with the other officer, showing the man his credentials. The officer was impressed and immediately gave up the young man's cell phone with the video.

Elisa and Vito watched the video, which showed a man and woman, hand in hand, strolling out of the park. She took the phone from Vito and watched it one more time. Then she clicked on the video and sent it to her phone by text attachment. Once she did that, she deleted any trace of her action, including the original video. She checked through the young man's pictures and videos and found nothing else with any evidence of the two people. Then she handed the phone back to the Polizia officer and left him with his young man.

Vito pulled Elisa aside and said, "You recognized someone in the video."

"Maybe," she said. "But if that person was involved, then it was a good shooting."

"How can you be sure?"

She didn't answer that. But she was. It was clearly Jake Adams in the video, and what she had to assume was his girlfriend. What in the hell was Jake up to? And how did he keep staying one step ahead of them?

17

Positano, Italy

Jake decided not to tell Russo about the bartender at the Royal Positano. Instead, he had given the Malavita capo an assignment in Naples—find out anyone and everyone associated with the man that Jake had been forced to kill in Pompeii. Russo could work his contacts and see if the dying man had told Jake the truth. Jake had given Russo a little lie. He had told the man that he needed some personal time with Alexandra, since she had not done anything exciting in months. He didn't tell the Mafia man about their child. Nor did he tell Russo where they were going.

The drive from Pompeii to the Amalfi Coast via Sorrento could take anywhere from forty minutes to a few hours, depending on traffic and weather. At least it was a sunny day and the off season for the coast, with a slight chill in the air. Jake had come to realize that

Italians could wear down jackets in June. Especially those in the south of Italy. Their blood ran cold.

With no location or name for this bartender at the Royal Positano Hotel, Jake and Alexandra had some time in the city until the bar opened that evening. So they wandered the narrow streets like the couple they really were, considering the purchase of shoes and leather goods. Jake was thankful that Alexandra was low maintenance and practical, only buying what she needed when she needed it. They could afford much more than they had, so Jake was the one who usually bought her more frivolous items.

Now they sat in a small café with a view of the sea a few blocks away, sipping fresh cups of cappuccino.

"We could just go to the hotel and ask for the name of the bartender," Alexandra said.

"No. They might tip her off and she'll bolt."

She nodded agreement.

"Besides," Jake said, "we don't know if the man was telling us the truth. He could have just made up the girl."

"I don't think so. A dying man does not think that way."

Perhaps, Jake thought.

"How do you want to play her?" she asked.

Good question. There was a time when Jake could use charm to extract information. But he guessed he had aged too much for that, especially if the woman was younger. "We'll have to assess the woman once we get there."

She checked her watch and fiddled with her phone.

"You want to call and check on Emma," Jake stated.

"I should."

Jake's phone buzzed and he pulled it from his pants to look who was calling him. This was the third time today Elisa had tried to call. She had obviously found the man he had killed at Pompeii. But after a few rings his phone would route her to some other location around the world randomly. One time it could be a tailor in Bangkok. Another time a Nevada brothel. He had programmed in fifty numbers, none of which had any affiliation with Jake.

"Are you gonna talk to that woman?" Alexandra asked. "I'll go outside and call Monica so you can speak with your old girlfriend in private." She didn't wait for Jake to respond. She just got up and left him there.

Jake answered his phone with a simple, "Yeah."

"I have tried to call you all day," Elisa said. "My calls keep getting routed to strange places."

"Really? It must be a glitch in the network."

"Right. More like a prank from a young boy. I spoke with a deli in Lima, a Chinese restaurant in Prague, and a bookstore in Oregon."

"Sounds like a strange combination," Jake said. "What can I do for you?"

"I'm in Pompeii." She paused.

"Good pizza."

"Dead body."

Yeah, he was right. She found him. Which meant their ploy with the man in Naples also worked. In reality, he needed her to remain one step behind him. Because when the shit hit the fan, she would be able to call in the cavalry.

"Sorry to hear that," Jake said. "But why are you investigating a dead body. You aren't with the Polizia."

"Because a certain man in Naples led us to a meeting place in the ruins at Pompeii. Of course we were late, since someone else beat us there."

"I think I told you that it's better to come late than to not come at all." All right. Now he was just messing with her, and he felt guilty for doing so.

"This is not a game, Jake."

Jake glanced outside, where Alexandra spoke into her phone, a smile on her face. He imagined that Emma might be on the other line making some kind of gurgling sound.

Back to his conversation, Jake said, "I'm sorry, Elisa."

"I have a video with you and your girlfriend on it leaving the ruins," she said with a whisper.

That wasn't possible. Russo had cut the feeds. "Must be a private video."

"Why? Because you somehow cut all of the video cameras for more than thirty minutes?"

She was good. But Jake knew that. "What do you want from me?"

"How about the truth? This is my country. If someone is planning an attack, I must know about it."

"All right. Someone is planning an attack."

"Who?"

"I'm trying to find out. I thought you had a man under surveillance."

"I told you he somehow disappeared in Bari. He could be anywhere in Italy by now." She paused and then said, "Did you kill this man in Pompeii?"

"You know that I would never kill someone who didn't try to kill me first." An answer without answering.

"I know," she agreed. "Did this man tell you anything before he died?"

Jake thought about that. He trusted Elisa with his life, but had no idea who she was currently working with, or if he could place his trust with someone he couldn't vet personally. "I trust you," Jake said. "But trust is earned."

She sighed heavy into the phone. "I know, Jake. But I can only officially work in Italy with my associate from AISI."

"Before I tell you anything else, let me vet the guy with my people," he said.

Alexandra came in and sat across from Jake again, her disposition placated by her Emma fix.

"All right," Elisa said. "I'll text you his data."

"Sounds good. Take care." Jake tapped off the call and shoved his phone into his pocket.

"Phone sex?" Alexandra asked.

"Right. I'm hard now." He knew she was kidding, since he had never told her about the brief affair he had experienced with Elisa years ago. She just knew they had worked an op together in Sicily years ago. "How is our little darling?"

Alexandra smiled. "Good. Except for one thing. She said her first word. Dada."

"Really? That's awesome."

"Right, because she referred to you."

"No. Because her first word wasn't fuck or shit."

Alexandra nodded agreement. Then she shifted back to their original conversation and said, "This Italian intel officer. What does she want?"

Before Jake could answer, his phone buzzed so he picked it up and read the text. It was the name of Elisa's associate at AISI, along with his agency identification number. Jake forwarded that text to his contact, Kurt Jenkins, the former Director of Central Intelligence. If anyone could vet this man, Kurt was the guy. He still had contacts and resources.

"What was that?" she asked.

"I told Elisa I wouldn't read her in on anything without first vetting her partner. I'm asking Kurt to help out."

"Sounds fair," she said, and then checked her watch. "Now you have two choices. We can check in to our hotel, or you can buy me a new pair of shoes."

"Hotel it is."

Crotone, Italy

Professor Antonio Baroni sat in his expansive office in the old building he owned on the outskirts of the ancient Greek old town. He swiveled in his chair and viewed his three large whiteboards, which contained his current work. The smallest board was used for current trivial problems, like his recent fascination with fresh ingredients for his meals, broken down to the molecular level. The second small board dealt with a problem with solar technology and global warming. But his largest board, that which took up most of one wall, illustrated his theory of government and how he could find a mathematical solution to human conduct. Although his area of specialty was with mathematics and physics, he felt that he had enough knowledge of the human condition to factor in behavior. He was, after all, human. At least he thought of himself that way. His only concern was one theory posited by scientists recently— that their entire reality was simply a simulation developed by a higher life form. How could he possibly factor in such an absurd notion? Or was it absurd?

There was a slight knock on his door, but he ignored it. He knew it was his associate, since that was the only man he had allowed to interrupt his thinking.

When he didn't answer, his associate came in followed by a dark man from the Middle East. Baroni's eyes shot up to his large whiteboard and he saw the factor he had used to represent this man.

Baroni swiveled in his chair and bore his gaze through the new man. "How was your travel from Athens?" They would speak in their only common language—English.

The man shuffled his feet, his eyes cast downward slightly. "I picked up a tail in Brindisi."

"What? Why was I not informed of this until now?" His shifted his gaze toward his trusted associate, Marco.

"I told no one until just now," the man from Athens said.

"Are you sure you lost the tail?" Baroni asked.

"Yes, sir. I bought a ticket to Rome in Brindisi, got off the train in Bari, and waited for the next train to Taranto. And then on to Crotone." The man smiled with his own cleverness.

Baroni needed this man and the others to strike his targets, to complete his vision. He guessed this person was not concerned with the mathematics of Baroni's vision. But his own agenda would be accomplished as well. A win for all parties involved. But he needed all of the pieces to fall into place, and that could have been a problem based on what happened earlier that morning in Pompeii. The eyes were removed from the equation, forcing him to vector in another direction. His cells were like living organisms. All of them had a purpose that led to sustained life. A malignancy could turn to cancer unless it was removed in its infancy. Failures had added up, with Geneva and Rome and Pompeii. Yet, these were minor setbacks. Unrelated pieces of a puzzle that could never be put together to form a coherent picture. This was a factor he was certain to be true.

"He must be tired from his journey," Baroni said. "Show him to his room, Marco."

His associate nodded and led the new man out into the living quarters.

Then Baroni swiveled his chair and cast his gaze once again upon the big board. All of the figures on the board came to life in his mind in a 3D holographic representation. Everything appeared to be working as planned, even with the minor setbacks. Intelligence was the only thing that mattered to Baroni. And his equation would reach fruition from theory to fact soon. Sooner than he had expected.

But he wished the Iraqi from Athens had been able to make contact with him in some way. After just a couple of hours of sleep, Baroni would have to put the man back on the train to Taranto to deliver a message for him in person. Then that person would contact his contact, and so on and so on. Soon, he knew, their little phone scheme would be compromised and everything would have to be done in person. That was all factored in to his equation.

18

Positano, Italy

Jake and Alexandra checked into the Royal Positano Hotel, which sat high on the hills of the Amalfi Coast with a splendid view of the city below. The hotel itself was nestled deep into the rocks. Every room on seven levels opened to a terrace with views of the city and sea. Yet, to anyone traveling by the hotel on the main road into the city, it did not appear like a hotel at all, since guests were required to walk down from the small parking lot to the hidden entrance below.

Both of them had rested for a while with the terrace doors open, the sound of birds chirping in the trees just out from the edge. Then they had made love, showered and dressed for the evening. Just before leaving their room, Jake got a call from Kurt Jenkins.

"Hello," Jake said. "What'd you find out about our friend?"

"Vito Galati's family comes from old money in northern Italy," Kurt said. "Some say all the way back to the Etruscans. He did his time in the Army before going to college, where he studied mathematics and political science."

"An odd combination," Jake said.

"That's what I thought. But I hear his parents expect him to eventually get into politics. They weren't happy when he joined the Internal Information and Security Agency after college."

"How has he done as an AISI officer?"

"Outstanding. He's a big-time riser in their agency. Everyone expects great things from him."

Now the most important question. "Can he be trusted?"

"I don't know," Kurt said. "Perhaps as much or less as anyone else."

"I don't like people with too much personal ambition," Jake said. "It makes folks do things for the wrong reasons."

"I know that about you, Jake. But I think you can give this young man a break."

Jake thanked his old friend for the information and then clicked off the call.

"What does Jenkins think?" Alexandra asked.

"Trust but verify."

"I've heard that before from you," she said.

"At this stage in my life, that's about all I've got left. Are you ready to get something to eat?"

"I could devour a Napoli pizza. And a beer or two."

Cheaper than shoes, Jake thought as they left the room.

The hotel restaurant and bar sat a couple of levels above their room. They got there at opening and the only people there were a large group of older patrons that resembled those German tourists from Pompeii earlier in the day. But Jake quickly picked up their language. It was Swedish.

The large terrace was wide open, but Jake didn't like the visibility to the bar from there. Instead, he found them a table with a view of the front entrance and the bar, with potential escape out the terrace if needed.

As they drank their beers and ate their pizzas, Jake kept his eyes on the bar. But there was just one bartender and that was a young skinny man.

"What do you think?" Alexandra asked.

Jake saw that the Swedish tourists had given way to a number of others as they ate. He checked his watch and realized that more staff might be needed as it got later.

"Let's go into the bar. Use your Russian persona."

She smiled. "That's an old one."

He got up and led the way into the bar. When Alexandra was with German Intelligence, she often used a Russian persona, Alexandra Bykofsky. Jake had first met her under that name in Austria more than a decade ago. Her Russian was flawless, and her accent while speaking English sent the blood flowing to all the right places in Jake.

Jake found two seats on the far end of the bar with his back to the wall and a view of the entrance to the restaurant. He ordered each of them a shot of Sambuca.

Alexandra spoke to Jake in Russian and smiled at the young bartender.

"What did she say?" the bartender asked in Italian.

Shrugging, Jake said in Italian, "She said it was getting busy in here, so she would enjoy watching you scramble behind the bar."

The bartender smiled and slid their clear shots across the bar to them. "I should have help, but someone called in sick."

Alexandra gave the man a confused look.

In German, Jake explained what the bartender said. Alexandra responded and then smiled.

"What did she say?" the bartender asked again.

"You don't want to know," Jake said. "*Sprechen Sie Deutsch?*"

"No."

"*Parli inglese?*"

"Yes, a little," the bartender said.

"I don't speak Russian," Jake lied. "We both speak German and a little English. I'm trying to teach her Italian. Anyway, she said she could bounce a Euro coin off your tight ass."

Now the young bartender blushed, smiled and walked away.

Jake whispered into Alexandra's ear in German, "I think he likes you. Why don't you head to the bathroom and I'll see how he reacts."

Alexandra smiled and sucked down the last of her Sambuca before getting down from the bar stool and putting an extra shake in her strut as she headed toward the bathroom.

Jake watched the bartender, who definitely noticed Alexandra's departure. He waved over the bartender, who lifted his chin and came quickly.

"Are you sure the other bartender can't make it in tonight?" Jake asked him.

The bartender leaned in and said, "I don't think she is sick. She sounded fine on the phone."

"If I could convince her to come to work, you could take a break and come to our room."

"You are staying here?"

"Yes."

The bartender thought it over and said, "I don't sleep with men."

"Good to know. Neither do I. But I do like to watch."

That seemed to be all right, based on the man's expression and the nod of his head.

"Does she live in Positano?" Jake asked.

"Just two blocks away."

"Give me her address and let me have a talk with her. Maybe she could come in for an hour."

The bartender quickly scribbled an address on a piece of paper and handed it to Jake.

He memorized the address and then said, "What's her name?"

The bartender gave Jake her first and last name. As he saw Alexandra coming back from the bathroom, he got up and met her in the middle of the bar. He whispered, "The bartender gave up the woman. Two blocks from here. I'll go check her out."

"She might be less intimidated by me," Alexandra said.

She had a good point. A woman was much more likely to let a strange woman in to her apartment at night.

Jake agreed and handed her the note. Then he gave her the name as well.

Alexandra turned and headed out through the restaurant toward the elevator.

Wandering back to the bar, Jake took a seat and waved over the bartender.

"You better get me a beer," Jake said. "She's going to go get your friend. I hope she speaks English."

"Better than me," the bartender said.

Curious, Jake asked, "What does the bartender look like?"

The Italian found his phone and pulled up a photo of the female bartender. She was a dark brunette with striking features.

"Damn it," Jake said.

"What?"

"My girlfriend also likes women. She might want to ask this woman to bed instead."

The bartender looked disappointed.

"Don't worry," Jake said. "I'll convince her to screw you."

The bartender's disposition improved as he wandered away and wiped the bar. "We could just text or call the other bartender."

"No," Jake said. "Some things are more convincing in person."

The bartender nodded agreement.

Jake sipped his beer. Then he pulled out his phone and typed up a text message to Elisa. He was willing to bring her in, along with her AISI friend. They could meet him in the morning at nine at the café near the sea in Positano. A few seconds later and he got his response. Elisa thanked him profusely. She'd be there.

•

Alexandra walked casually up to the road that led down toward the city center of Positano. Then she started to descend toward a row of apartments that sat on the upper side of the road. After leaving the bar where

Jake had pretended to pimp her out to the bartender, she had first gone down to their room and swapped out her pocket pistol .380 with six rounds for her larger 9mm Glock with 17 rounds, hidden in an underarm sling on her left side and covered with her leather jacket.

She had no idea if this woman was a radical or just a cog in the communications chain. But she wasn't about to take a chance.

Finding the address, she hiked up a set of narrow steps between two buildings until she reached a small terrace landing with a couple of doors. Considering her approach, she thought she'd try something different. Women, even in this sedate Amalfi Coast community, still didn't like coming to the door, especially at night. Yet, she also knew that people were generally accommodating. They liked to think they were open to others—even though those others might try to rape or murder them.

Alexandra knocked lightly on the door and tried her best not to look intimidating. Which could be a problem for a former intelligence officer. By nature, she knew, she could come across as brusque.

When she saw motion at the peep hole, she smiled at the person behind the door.

The door opened slowly and a sliver of light seeped through, along with a left eye.

"If you are looking for Marco, he moved a month ago," the woman said in Italian.

"Tell Marco I'll cut his balls off." Alexandra knew she couldn't bluff the approach, since the dying man had not given them that much. So she played drunken ex-girlfriend. "Are you his new whore?"

"I told you that Marco has moved."

Alexandra pretended to almost throw up. Then she recovered and said, "That's a lie, bitch. You're cute. I'll give that much. Does he try to take you up the ass? I think he might be secretly gay."

"I don't know Marco," she said. "I just get some of his mail."

"Seriously? Where did he move?"

"I don't know," the woman said.

By now the woman had opened the door a little more, showing that she had no security chain. With one swift move, Alexandra shoved her shoulder into the door, knocking the much smaller woman back a few feet. Before the woman could react, Alexandra had her gun out and pointed at the woman's face.

Closing the door and locking it behind her, Alexandra said, "You might want to take a seat." She went from drunk to sober instantaneously.

The woman was afraid, no doubt. She started to shift back to comply, but then with a sudden quickness, she rushed Alexandra and hit her in the stomach, knocking her back into the wall. Then the woman started to wail on Alexandra, striking her with both fists like a wild woman. But the blows were not doing much damage against Alexandra's large frame. As the woman moved in quickly for another round, Alexandra shoved her right elbow up, contacting the woman's chin hard and knocking the woman out instantly.

Alexandra shook her head as the woman lay at her feet unconscious. She found her phone and texted Jake, saying she was at the woman's apartment and he should come immediately.

·

Jake looked at his text and shook his head. What did that mean? Alexandra was more than capable of interrogating the woman.

'Is everything all right?' Jake texted.

'Fine. She's under the weather.'

He knew what that meant. Alexandra had been forced to subdue the woman.

He glanced at the bartender, who came over and asked if everything was going as planned.

"Everything is perfect," Jake said. "But your friend was not lying. She is not feeling well. However, why don't you just come to our room when you get off work?"

"That works for me," the bartender said.

Jake gave the man the room number. But not theirs.

He paid for the drinks with cash and wandered out of the building. He quickly found the woman's apartment and Alexandra met him at the door. Jake immediately saw the woman tied to a chair in the kitchen area, her head slumped to her left shoulder.

"Jesus. Did you kill her?"

"I barely hit her. She has a glass jaw."

"Did you find anything important here?"

"I was busy tying her up."

Jake started searching the woman's small apartment. During the search, he noticed that the woman started to wake from her slumber. Alexandra had done a good job tying and gagging the woman, so he continued to search. But, if the woman had half a brain, she would not have any evidence of her activity written down anywhere.

While Jake checked for anything physical, Alexandra searched through the woman's laptop computer and her cell phone. Most people forgot to clear their text entries or internet histories. Only those who had something to hide scrubbed those clean. But those were never really gone. The Agency could easily find every site she had ever visited online. Jake didn't think they had time for that, though. He did have an idea that might work. He whispered his plan to Alexandra.

Jake would speak only German and Alexandra would use only Russian. They would start with innocuous questions asking where she kept it—not being specific about what it might be. Then, when they got frustrated, they would try to piece some simple Italian together. When she was eventually turned over to the Italians, she would swear that a German man and a Russian woman had tortured her. But Jake didn't think it would come to torture. This woman seemed to be a simple courier or intermediary. All they needed from her was her contact up the chain. First, though, they would get her to divulge the name they already knew—the name of the man Jake had shot at the Pompeii ruins that morning. By now, Jake guessed, she would have to know that this man was dead and out of commission. That's why she really called in sick. He could tell that as soon as he stepped into her bedroom. She was packing. Ready to run.

Jake walked over to the woman, who was now bright eyed and stretching against the lamp cord Alexandra had used to tie her. He grasped her shirt and ripped it from top to bottom, exposing her modest breasts in a pushup bra. First rule of interrogation? Treat the suspect like shit. Like they were just a piece of meat. He found a kitchen knife and came back to the woman, whose eyes were wide with fear. Moving the knife across the woman's face near her eyes, Jake then slid the blade along her thin neck and across her collar bone. Her breathing increased, and Jake thought the woman might pass out with fear. Then Jake slid the blade under the center of the woman's bra and cut the bra off, exposing her breasts. He slipped the blade across one erect nipple and then the other one. Okay, he thought, now she knew where he would start. She was ready.

19

Padua, Italy

The train pulled into the station in early morning after traveling from Innsbruck. The sun was just rising over the Adriatic and Venice to the east.

Derrick Konrad had just woken from a light sleep in his private sleeper car as the train came to a gentle stop at the Padua Central Train Station.

Padua, or more appropriately Padova, was a major university city—where Galileo had once taught physics and developed the truth that the Earth revolved around the sun and not the other way around. A fact that the church called heresy and allowed them to imprison the brilliant scientist who had invented the telescope.

Holgar rushed into the cabin and said, "We have to go."

"Why?"

"Our man has his bag and is on the move off the train."

Konrad grabbed his bag and slung it over his shoulder. Then the two of them pushed out through the various passengers gawking out the windows at the terminal. The train, along with their tickets, was scheduled to terminate in Venice. So, not many were getting off. Which could be a problem. They would be noticed, Konrad realized.

"Split up," Konrad said to his young associate.

Holgar nodded understanding.

They were barely able to step off the train before it pulled away toward Venice. Konrad spotted their target ahead, making his way toward the front entrance of the station. He would take the lead first, while Holgar stayed back and observed both from a distance.

Instead of picking up a taxi, the man they had followed from Geneva walked south toward the center of the city along *Corso de Popolo*. After a block, Konrad stepped into a building and let Holgar take the lead. They did this a couple of more times until they reached the bridge over the river and the road became Corso de

Giuseppe Garibaldi. A block after the bridge, their subject crossed the street and entered a park which led to one of the city's most famous churches, the *Cappella degli Scrovegni*. Konrad had been here once on a trip years ago in gymnasium school, where they had traveled to view important works of Renaissance art. His mind traveled back to those simpler days and how he didn't at the time truly appreciate the beautiful frescos on the wall of the chapel by Giotto, painted around 1303. How did he remember that? Focus, Derrick.

His subject made a direct approach to the chapel and went inside.

Konrad got a call on his cell and he picked up but continued to walk. "Yeah."

"Do you want to go in there?" Holgar asked.

Glancing across the street, he saw his partner walking and tried not to look at Konrad.

"No," Konrad said. "I've been in there. There's nowhere he can go."

"He could be meeting with someone."

Good point. But at this hour the chapel would not have many tourists checking out the frescos. So there was no way they could blend in.

"Cross the road ahead and cover any possible retreat in that direction," Konrad said. "He might just be an art lover. He could double back and pick up the next train to Venice. Many people do that."

"Will do. Is it impressive?"

"It's worth a look. It's not the Sistine Chapel, but a close second." What was this man up to, Konrad wondered? Then he stopped and turned without warning, a technique he had learned from an older man with INTERPOL. When he did so, a man about a block away nearly stopped, but then he started to walk again as if nothing had happened. Crap! "We've got a problem."

Ahead, Holgar was crossing the street, which gave him a reason to glance back toward Konrad. "What?"

"A man about a block behind me. He's tailing me?"

"I see him. Are you sure?"

"Yes. I'll hold tight here and pretend to look at a map on my phone." He clicked off the call and pulled up a map of his current location. Then he swiveled around to try to orient himself with the map, making the screen larger with his fingers.

By now the man he thought was following him was almost upon him. Konrad had one more play. As the guy got closer, Konrad switched quickly back to his camera, firing off a series of shots, capturing the man. Then he went back to the map.

The tail was now upon him. He was a man in his 50s who could have been Italian or someone from the Balkans. "Excuse me," Konrad said in his best English. "Could you tell me where to find St. Anthony Basilica?"

The tail hesitated, his eyes intense. "*Non Capisco*."

Now Konrad tried on a southern accent from America. "Crap on toast. I know that doggone sucker is somewhere hereabouts. Are you sure?"

The man shrugged.

Then, in broken Italian, Konrad asked, "I'm looking for *La Basilica di Sant'Antonio di Padova*?" He intentionally butchered the name of the city's famous basilica.

Now, the man looked at Konrad's phone and lifted his chin with understanding. His tail spoke in Italian, explaining that the basilica wasn't far from here. Then the man wandered down the street. But Konrad had gotten what he needed—a photo of the tail, and the fact that the man spoke Italian with a Slavic accent. What the hell was going on?

His phone buzzed and he checked his incoming text. Holgar was looking for guidance. Konrad texted back, telling him to go to the far eastern side of the chapel park. He didn't need an answer, though, since he could see Holgar move off toward that location. While he was on his phone, he checked on the series of photos he had taken of his tail—if the man was truly following him. He found the best image and texted it to his boss at INTERPOL, giving him the details of where he was and his status.

Seconds later, just as his subject exited the chapel, he got a text back from INTERPOL saying 'This man is from Serbia. He has a Red Notice on him for kidnapping, murder, and crimes against humanity. Bring him in.'

Konrad thought he had recognized the man from somewhere. He texted back, 'He is gone.'

But the man wasn't gone, he was still ahead walking slowly down the *Corso de Giuseppe Garibaldi*. It was a judgment call, and Konrad hoped he had made the right call. He had a feeling the subject he had followed from Geneva was more important than an old war criminal from the Balkan War. Besides, there was no way that this Serb was here by chance. He was involved. More importantly, Konrad was certain the man had burned him. He had obviously been at the Padua train station charged with following their subject to make sure he wasn't being followed. Which he was. Maybe he should just make the arrest now. But which man? The one he suspected was planning a bombing in Europe? Or a man who had an INTERPOL Red Notice already on him, and was wanted by the International Court of Justice in The Hague?

Konrad knew one thing for certain. He needed more assets.

20

Positano, Italy

It didn't take Jake and Alexandra long to get the entirety of what they thought the bartender knew about the part she played in the network planning to strike Italy. Jake had been right. Whoever was running the show was using a precise calculation for each member on each rung of the ladder. Nobody knew more than they needed to know to accomplish their mission.

They ate a scant breakfast at the hotel, drinking a decent cappuccino. But they checked out by 0845 and drove down the hill toward the seafront to meet Italian Intelligence Officer Elisa Murici at the same café Jake and Alexandra had been to the day before, arriving at precisely 0900.

Elisa was already sitting inside with a young man with long curly hair nearly to his shoulders. Jake thought the guy looked like a model for some high-end clothing line.

Jake and Elisa kissed on both cheeks, but he only shook the young man's hand, making sure to lay down a solid grip. Alexandra had still not gotten into the whole kiss greeting, despite their long stay in Italy. Her staunch German ancestry wouldn't allow it, Jake guessed. But she was cordial with Elisa and her associate, a man named Vito Galati.

They ordered cappuccinos all around and made small talk about the current weather until they came, all four with a different drawing in the foam. Vito was a talker, his English quite good. When they switched to Italian periodically, Vito seemed a bit confused.

"What's the matter?" Jake asked the young officer with AISI.

"Your Italian is quite good," Vito said. "It seems to be infused with local Calabrese."

"It should," Elisa said. "That's where Jake has been living for the last couple of years."

"The Calabrese are good people," Vito said. "They will do anything for you."

"They are nice," Jake said, "but don't piss them off."

"Like the Malavita?" Vito asked.

"Family in general," Jake corrected. Then he considered not saying something, but he pushed forward anyway. He needed to make sure this guy knew that he knew who he was dealing with, and was not just some former CIA officer. "Not everyone can trace their heritage back to the Etruscans. But many in Calabria can at least go back to their Greek ancestry."

When Jake mentioned the Etruscans, Vito's eyes widened. He said, "You have done your homework, Mister Adams. I'm afraid you have me at a disadvantage."

Jake doubted that, unless Elisa was keeping his background secret for a reason. He glanced at Elisa, who gave him a nearly imperceptible nod. So he gave the man a brief bio—Air Force officer, CIA, private security consultant. That was enough to impress the Italian.

Vito tried to hold back a smile when he said, "Was the Air Force flying bi-planes back then?"

"Yeah, and you were probably swimming around in your father's balls when I was fighting the Communists," Jake said, keeping things light with a smile of his own.

"Boys," Alexandra said, "I'm sure you all have enormous cocks."

"At least one of us," Vito said. "I can't vouch for my American friend."

The Italian didn't know that Jake had also slept with his partner. Neither did Alexandra. Time to change the subject.

"Do you want to know what happened in Pompeii?" Jake asked, and then took a long sip of his cappuccino.

Elisa nodded.

Vito shrugged.

Jake explained, first backing up to their original operation in Rome, the second op in Rome, including the various shootings, the shift to Naples, and then finally their little adventure in Pompeii. For now he left out the bartender. Then he finished his cappuccino.

"Interesting," Elisa said. "But why are you here on the Amalfi?"

"It's a beautiful coast," Jake said. "I've been meaning to take Alexandra here for a while."

He could tell by Elisa's expression that she wasn't buying it. He forgot how good she was at ready people. But he guessed that she could read him better than most, considering the intimacy of their relationship.

"What are we doing here, Jake?" Elisa asked.

"You wanted to be read in on my activities," Jake said. "I'm only doing this because we are friends. I'm not under any obligation to tell you anything."

Vito jumped in head first. "But I'm with AISI. You have been involved with a number of murders in Italy. That is my business."

Jake shifted forward in his chair toward the young man. "Murders? Justified self defense. Maybe if you did your damn job, the crime rate wouldn't be so high in Italy."

"I can see the bulge under your left arm," Vito said. "I believe you are not authorized to carry a concealed handgun in Italy."

The young man was partially correct. Jake had been given a special license to carry a handgun in Austria and Germany. However, with the open borders policy of the EU, those licenses extended to every country in the European Union. Also, he had a special two-year license to carry in Italy as a private security officer. His benefactor, the billionaire Carlos Gomez, had made that happen with little red tape.

"When a man pulls a gun on me and tries to blow my head off," Jake said, "I only have one thing on my side—and that's my God-given right to self defense. We have a saying in America. It's better to be judged by twelve than carried by six. I think that works in Italy as well."

Elisa finished her cappuccino and set her cup down onto the saucer with force. "Guys. We are all on the same side. Jake is authorized to carry a gun in Italy." Then she turned to her young associate and said, "Wait for me outside."

This wasn't a request, and the AISI officer shook his head as he rose, considering if he should protest. Instead, he stormed out the door and crossed the street, soaking in the morning sun as he gazed out at the sea.

"We need to talk," Elisa said to Jake, but her eyes shifted toward Alexandra.

Finishing her cappuccino, Alexandra took the hint and left Jake and Elisa alone. Jake watched as his girlfriend crossed the street and stood next to Vito.

"What's going on, Jake?" she asked.

"What do you mean?" He knew what she meant.

"You have left me bread crumbs across Italy, only letting me have table scraps when you desire. Now, I appreciate what little help you have given me, but your lack of professional cooperation is confusing. I thought we had a good relationship."

She had a damn good point. He had always had a problem playing well with others, especially during his time with the Agency. But once he went private, his level of trust was restricted even more. He said nothing.

Elisa continued, "I don't know who you're working for, but I'm guessing you still have some pull, otherwise you wouldn't have been able to get background intel on Vito so quickly."

"I don't think I can work with that young punk," Jake said. "He's an arrogant bastard."

"Because he reminds you of a younger you?"

"I don't recall you having such an acute sense of humor."

"Sometimes the truth is hard to accept," she said.

They stared at each other for a moment, and Jake's mind drifted back a few years when they stayed at a hotel overlooking the Med in Sicily. They had been good together. And that was the problem.

"What?" she asked. "You're thinking about something."

Yeah, he remembered Elisa being the aggressor in their first encounter, coming out of her shower completely naked. How could he have refused her then? With her fine body, that was impossible.

"I was thinking about staying at that sleazy hotel in Sicily, where you patched up my bullet wound with Sambuca, thread and glue."

"And how I damn near raped you after fixing you?"

"I know. I felt so cheap."

She smiled. "You didn't seem to complain." Elisa hesitated and then added, "I hear you got shot in the Baltics recently."

"I got shot in the stomach," he said. "Are you checking up on me?"

"I hear things."

"Such as?"

"That you have a new daughter."

It wasn't like Jake had kept that a complete secret. He had used his real name on Emma's birth certificate. "And?"

"I heard that Toni died not too long ago. I was sorry to hear that. I know you two had great history. Do you know she was awarded the Order of Merit of the Italian Republic posthumously for her service for so many years in Italy?"

"No, I didn't know that."

"It was a private ceremony, of course."

Wow, a Knight of the Italian Republic. Jake had a similar honor bestowed upon him in Austria years ago.

"I heard Toni had a son," Elisa said. "But I didn't find out until after the ceremony. I tried to get you to come, but you were unavailable. We would still like to get the medal and certificate to her son. Your son, I'm guessing."

"I had no idea until a couple of years ago," Jake assured her. "She gave her child to her sister to raise."

"If I get these to you, could you make sure he gets the award? We also have a video of the ceremony."

"He would like that. So would Toni's sister. Is this what you wanted to discuss with me alone?"

She let out a breath of air, her eyes shifting toward her partner and Alexandra outside. "Partly. I understand you are working with a capo in the Calabrese Malavita."

Jake said nothing.

"As you know, that's a dangerous proposition."

"Not as dangerous has having multiple terrorist cells poised to strike across Italy. Remember, despite their bad deeds, the Malavita are still loyal Italians."

"I know. But I'm not sure you should trust them."

Jake shifted his head toward her partner out on the street. "What makes you think I can trust wonder boy?"

"Do you trust me?"

"Of course."

"Then you have your answer."

Now she needed to get down to the real reason for their meeting, he thought. But he waited for her to divulge that to him.

She said, "It's embarrassing that I lost the man in Bari. I need you to help me find him."

"How?"

Elisa leaned toward Jake and whispered, "I was able to place a tracker on the guy while on the ferry crossing from Greece."

Jake was confused. "Then why in the hell are you not tracking him down?"

"Two reasons," she said. "First, I requested the trace through my agency and they said the device was no longer working."

"And you don't believe them," Jake said.

"That's right. It's a load of crap. Which brings me to my second point. Something is going on at the highest levels of my government that is disturbing."

"Like what?"

"I don't know. It's almost like they want to get hit by terrorists."

"What? Why?"

She shrugged.

That made no sense. Why would a government want terrorists to blow shit up, killing innocent people? Like most of the other European governments, the Italians seemed to be asleep at the wheel. They all reminded Jake of the three monkeys—see no evil, hear no evil, and speak no evil. But evil existed in this world, and Jake knew the only way to solve that problem was to kill it.

"You have the device code?" Jake asked.

She glanced about, especially at her partner outside, and then pulled out a piece of paper. Jake immediately knew the device she had used. It was the smallest GPS tracking unit ever developed. It was so small that it could be added to someone's food and ingested. Of course, that only worked if the person didn't crunch down on it with his teeth, or if it didn't end up down the toilet too soon.

Jake quickly took a photo of the spec code and attached it to a text to Kurt Jenkins, along with a brief but cryptic explanation. ASAP, Jake insisted.

"How did you place the device?" Jake asked.

"The man had to sleep sometime," she said. "It's hidden within a pocket on his backpack."

"Nice work."

"Now," she said, "one more thing. The man you killed in Pompeii. What did he tell you? You aren't in Positano for the view."

Smiling, Jake explained his encounter with the bartender the night before, leaving out the gory details.

"And she told you her contact was from Calabria?" Elisa asked.

"That's right."

"Where in Calabria? That's a big place."

"We're not sure," he said. "Which is why we're still here. Well, that and the fact that I promised to meet you this morning."

She looked confused. "Where did you put the woman?"

"First of all, how did you know we were working with the Malavita?"

"The bread crumbs you left me," she said. "There were ties to organized crime."

"That was on purpose," he said. "I wanted you to know that they were not the ones planning an attack. Now, why didn't you want your partner to hear all of this?" Jake came to the answer on his own. "You don't trust him either."

"No comment."

He could tell that she was struggling with something internally. Trust was a bitch in the intelligence game, he knew. There were only a handful of people Jake ever trusted with his life. And most of those were either retired or dead now.

"The woman," she said. "Where is she?"

"I turned her over to our Agency folks from Rome, along with her laptop." He smiled.

"But you held something back."

"She tried to erase her contact's number from her phone, but I found it. Then I got rid of the phone."

"Did you trace the number?"

"Still waiting to hear back."

Jake glanced out to the street again, seeing that Alexandra was heavily engaged with the young Italian. Just then a car rolled up and hit the brakes. Diving across the table, Jake caught Elisa at the same time that the glass from the front window smashed in, sending shards flying everywhere. The sounds of automatic gunfire echoed through the café and patrons screamed. It was chaos.

21

Jake found himself on top of Elisa, their faces just inches apart. His ears were ringing, an all too familiar experience for him.

Then he heard screaming and Jake rolled to his side, his gun out and pointed toward the sound. His eyes focused and he realized Alexandra was doing the screaming.

"Are you all right?" Alexandra asked.

Getting up from the floor, Jake helped Elisa up. "Where are they?"

"They drove away," Alexandra said. "I got off a couple of rounds. But I don't know if I hit anyone."

Jake glanced at the young AISI officer and said, "What about you?"

"I got the license number," Vito said. "I called it in."

"Great. The car will come up stolen," Jake said. "Anybody hurt in here?" He glanced about the room, but most of the patrons were still cowering under tables or behind the pastry counter. Jake holstered his gun and covered it with his leather jacket.

Elisa moved about the café asking if anyone was hurt. It appeared that they had all gotten lucky.

"We need to get moving," Jake said to Alexandra. "Get the car."

Alexandra nodded and left.

Jake observed the young AISI officer, who looked like a deer in the headlights. "Hey, kid. Get your head together."

"What?" Vito asked.

"We need to go. We can't stay here to talk with the local Polizia."

"But I have a responsibility," the young man said, but he was clearly unsure of himself.

Jake waved Elisa over. "We need to get the hell out of here. And we'll need your identification to do so."

He escorted the two Italians outside and the three of them piled into the car Alexandra had just driven to the front entrance. "Get in the front with her," Jake ordered Vito. "And get your identification ready. The Polizia will have the roads closed above."

That was the problem with the Amalfi Coast. There was only one major winding road that connected each little hillside town nestled in the hills overlooking the sea.

Alexandra pushed the gas and they lurched up the hill toward the main road. At the top of the hill, she said, "Which way?"

"Right toward Salerno," Jake said from the back seat.

"Sorrento might be easier," Elisa said.

Jake pointed to the right. "That's why we go the other way. That's the way the shooters will go."

Cranking the wheel and hitting the gas, Alexandra accelerated through the gears taking the corners with too much speed. But there were no cars coming from the other direction. Jake knew these roads. There was always traffic in both directions on these narrow roads. But nothing approached from the other direction.

"They've blocked the road ahead," Jake said.

"Maybe we should pull back and explain what happened," Vito said. "It was clearly a Malavita tactic. And what about our car?"

Jake pulled his gun and placed the barrel at the base of the young officer's head. "Who the fuck did you tell you were coming to Positano?"

Vito, feeling the cold metal, tried to turn his head but felt the force of Jake's gun and continued looking forward.

"Jake," Elisa said. "Stop it."

"Not until he answers the question."

"I followed procedure," Vito said. "When we left our hotel this morning in Pompeii, I told my boss about our meeting."

"My God," Jake said. "You're a perfect kind of stupid."

"What? That's what I was trained to do." Sweat built up on the young man's forehead. He had obviously never had a gun pointed at him. He was probably still in shock from the shooting.

Jake pulled back his gun but didn't return it to the holster. "Then you've got a problem with your agency."

"That's impossible," Vito said. Finally, he turned to look at Jake. But his eyes said everything. The man wasn't only in shock. He was coming to realize that Jake might be right. "What about your side?"

Shaking his head, Jake said, "We didn't tell anyone about the meeting." Then he glanced at Elisa for her response.

Elisa shook her head. "I haven't checked in with my agency since I started working with Vito and AISI."

"People," Alexandra said, hitting the brakes. "We've got a problem."

Looking ahead on the road, Jake could see what had been a road block with two Polizia cars, their red and blue lights flashing. A line of cars was piling up on the back side of the road block, and three cars remained on their side. But one of the Polizia cars was jacked sideways. Someone had busted through the roadblock.

"Push through," Jake said.

Alexandra moved the car around those on their side and barely squeezed between the two Polizia cars. The two Polizia officers were on the ground with multiple bullet holes, blood seeping out onto the pavement. The cars piling up on the other side of the road block seemed to be frozen in time, with zombies behind the wheel. Those close to the front were afraid. As they passed the newly arrived, they simply looked concerned and confused.

Once they got through the road block, Alexandra picked up speed again.

Jake guessed the two Polizia officers had not been able to call in the shooting. That meant there would probably not be a road block ahead. At least not for a while, until they figured out their perimeter had been breached.

"Now what?" Vito asked.

Jake's phone buzzed. He put his gun into its holster under his left arm and then found his phone. It was a message from Kurt Jenkins. He was able to locate the cell phone of the bartender's contact. It was still on and just pinged from a cell tower. Jake thanked his old friend. Then he tapped on the address and mapped the location.

"What is it?" Elisa asked Jake.

"A direction." He leaned forward toward Alexandra. "Head toward Salerno and get on the Autostrada heading south."

Then he leaned back and turned to Elisa. "The bartender's contact."

"Do you have a name?" she asked.

"He's running that for me now. He'll get back with me soon."

"Good." Elisa considered her words carefully, her eyes shifting toward her young partner in the front seat. "If there's a problem, we'll find it, Jake."

"I understand," he said.

"What about your Malavita friend?"

Jake shook his head. "He's in Naples running down a few things for me. He has no idea we're even on the Amalfi Coast."

"And your Agency friend?" she asked.

"Is beyond trustworthy. I've worked with him for more than twenty years. The leak is on your side."

Elisa gave him a knowing nod. "As I mentioned before, something strange is going on."

Jake had to agree. There was no way that the young officer could have tipped off the shooters. There was no way he could have known he wouldn't have been in the café himself. Elisa had told Vito to step outside. Otherwise he too would have been in the line of fire. Nobody is stupid enough to call in a strike on his own position.

22

Crotone, Italy

Professor Antonio Baroni stood before a full-length mirror observing himself from top to bottom. Although he had not historically considered his appearance, he noticed now that his left ear stuck out more than his right ear. And he had done a rather poor job trimming his gray goatee. The right side came in too far. Perhaps subconsciously he was overcompensating for his ears being out of alignment. Now he traced the lines around his eyes and tried to remember the jokes that had led to such craters forming. He fully understood the horizontal lines of consternation that streaked across his forehead. Each of those represented a difficult equation he had taken too long to discover. He felt another line forming at this moment, based almost entirely on the news he had just gotten from his protégé less than an hour ago. Disturbing news. A number of his cells seemed to be collapsing. Disappearing actually. Then there was the man coming from Geneva, which had been a truly colossal debacle. Word had come in that the only man to escape from Switzerland was now being followed by someone in Padova, where he himself had once taught physics and mathematics. He truly admired Galileo Galilei. But his passion was with the Pythagoreans, which is why he had come to Crotone to begin with, where Pythagoras had once taught and established his theorem.

Now he had a phone call to make to his contact in the Italian government. A former student of his at the University of Padova.

He picked up his cell phone and found his contact. Then he waited.

Finally, his contact picked up. "Yes."

"What is going on?" Baroni asked.

"What do you mean?"

"I mean precisely that. You are paid to provide information." This was true, but it also helped that Baroni knew certain things about his contact that would be quite embarrassing if disclosed to the press or his superiors. And now the man was in too deep to get out, since Baroni kept meticulous records of their activities. Down to the precise minute. Everything calculated and plugged into his whiteboard.

"I can only give you what I know," the man said. His tone was nearly desperate.

Baroni still needed this man, so he had to come across as curious and a little disappointed, but not angry enough to take it out on the contact or his family. "And Positano?"

"The level of success there was not predetermined. Our information was good, but the method they used to achieve their goal was not. . .superior."

To say the least. "Are you certain those were the people responsible for taking down our eyes in Rome?"

"Yes. And those in Naples and Pompeii."

This was disturbing. "Who are they?"

"Other than our people," the man said, "we are not entirely certain. We just have reports of a man and a woman who speak multiple languages."

"Such as?"

"Russian, German, Italian and English. So far. But they have certain skills that indicate they are intelligence officers or law enforcement. Perhaps military intelligence."

"From which country?"

"That is the question I am trying to discover. But there is also a wild card. A man from the Malavita."

"Are you sure?"

"Yes. Upon our debrief with the man from Naples, he confirmed that fact."

The Malavita nearly controlled all of Calabria. Although they could be brutal, their motivations were usually economic. They were like a band of Robin Hoods. Only they took from companies and private wealthy citizens, through kidnappings and extortion, and lined their own pockets. Which is why the average citizen in Calabria wasn't concerned about their activities. Nobody cared about illegal activity if it didn't have an impact on their daily life.

"Is there anything else I need to be aware of?" Baroni asked.

"Perhaps. I know nothing about your activities. But, considering current events, you might want to consider an accelerated timeline."

"I understand. I have already plugged that into my algorithm. Keep me informed. And find out who that man and woman are as soon as possible."

"Yes, sir."

He got off the phone and slipped it into his jacket pocket. Then he glanced into the mirror again and considered the lines on his forehead once more. He could almost see the dismay digging a new trench, like a speedy glacier cutting through a rocky landscape.

Yeah, the timeline was compromised, he knew. He was generally a patient man. Haste led to mistakes. But he had also planned for this potential setback.

23

Padua, Italy

Derrick Konrad wasn't a hundred percent certain that he had been burned by the chapel, but he was fairly certain. And perhaps that was enough. His boss in Switzerland had ordered him to take the Serb. The Red Notice on this man was one of the oldest in the INTERPOL system. How was this Serb related to the man they had tracked all the way from Geneva? Only a proper interrogation would reveal that. Yet, he also knew that once they picked up the Serb they would be forced almost immediately to turn him over to the authorities in The Hague. Assuming, of course, they knew the Serb had been captured. And that fact could be held back for a while.

Now, after following their subject around the city like a tourist, Konrad sat in the *Café Pedrocchi* near a massive marble column that could have sat in front of an ancient temple. This place was an iconic symbol of the city, built in 1831, and frequented by students from the second oldest university in Italy. Its elegance was nearly overwhelming to Konrad, who was having a hard time concentrating on his subject, the man he had followed from Geneva. Konrad had ignored orders to capture the Serb. At least for now.

His associate was outside somewhere coordinating with local authorities, but kept a comm line open.

"Is he still sitting there?" Holgar asked over the comm.

"Yes." With the high ceilings and the large expanse, his speech would not be noticed, since many others in the café were talking on their phones. Konrad had his phone up to his ear, but he was simply using it as a prop and occasionally taking photos surreptitiously. By now Konrad had enough photos of his potential dirtbag terrorist to fill an album.

What was this man up to? Did he know he was being followed?

His phone suddenly buzzed and he looked to see that it was an alarm reminder for him to take his medication. Because of his distraction with his work, he had forgotten all about it. He looked down at this left hand and saw a small tremor. Konrad quickly found his emergency pill that he kept in his shirt pocket and swallowed it without water. Then he used the last of his cappuccino to wash it down. Now he could only hope that he didn't end up on the decorative sepia marble floor flopping like a fish out of water.

"Derrick, Derrick. Answer."

"Say again," Konrad said.

"I said our Serbian friend is back. He's heading into the front door now."

Konrad saw the man stride confidently toward his location. What the hell was this man doing? The Serb still wore the long coat he had worn earlier that morning, but now he also had a backpack over his shoulder. Expecting the man to simply pass him, Konrad was shocked when the man pulled out a chair at the table across from him and sat down.

The Serb said something, but Konrad didn't understand him. Was that Serbian?

Konrad went to German. "I'm sorry. But I don't understand."

Smiling slightly, the Serb pulled his backpack from his shoulder and set it gently to the floor. "So, you are German?" the Serb asked.

"Yes. On vacation from Berlin," Konrad said, using a city he knew well, just in case the man was familiar with that place.

The Serb shook his head. "You are Polizei," the man said in perfect German. "Why are you following me?"

"I'm not following you. I think I saw you earlier today near the *Cappella degli Scrovegni*. And now here. Two of the most famous city landmarks."

"I know when I am being followed. Before you alert your partner outside, you must be aware that the backpack I just set down is filled with a significant amount of Semtex."

Konrad sat back in his chair, as if that extra distance would protect him from a blast from a backpack of plastic explosives. "What do you want?"

The Serb smiled again. "The man over my shoulder, the man you have followed since Geneva, will get up in a few seconds and walk out of the café. Your partner will not follow him."

"I don't understand."

"Very simple. He leaves and we stay here. Your partner doesn't follow him. If he does, I set off this bomb and blow this landmark into rubble. Look around. There must be fifty people in here. That is a lot of pink mist. The Polizia will have to spend weeks determining even how many were killed."

"Did you hear that?" Konrad said into his comm.

"Yes, sir," Holgar said. "What do we do?"

Before he could answer, Konrad watched as his subject got up from his table, slung his pack over his shoulder, and strolled casually out of the café.

"Let him go," Konrad said. Then he looked across the table at the Serb. "How do I know your backpack has a bomb?"

"Do you want to take that chance?"

A waiter came to the table, but the Serb simply waved him away.

This was a conundrum without a training scenario, Konrad thought. There was no way to counter the crazy man willing to blow himself up.

The Serb was stalling. Waiting for the subject to get away.

Konrad's jacket was open and part of him considered simply pulling his gun and shooting this Serb in the head. But what if the man was telling the truth and he had a dead man switch on the bomb? To the contrary, what if the man was bluffing. Then Konrad would have shot a potentially unarmed man in front of dozens of witnesses.

"What do you want?" Konrad asked the Serb.

"I would say world peace, but that would be a lie," the Serb said. "Anarchy is much more fun."

"You have a long-standing warrant on you," Konrad said, not wanting to mention the INTERPOL Red Notice, which would give the man too much information about him.

"So, you know who I am. Or you know who you think I am. Not everything you read is true."

"Says the terrorist who claims he has a bomb in his backpack. You're just misunderstood." Konrad was having a hard time containing his smartass disposition. But on a high note, his hands were no longer trembling. He was focused now.

The man looked at his watch and stood up, lifting the backpack as he rose. He slung the bag over his right shoulder and started to turn, but he stopped and said, "You Polizei are all like school bullies. You think you have all the answers. Yet, you only know a fraction of what goes on in this world. A storm is coming and you will all be without shelter. Strap yourself in for the ride."

The Serb turned and walked toward the front door. Konrad didn't want to panic the patrons, so he simply got up and started following the Serb.

"He's heading toward the front door," Konrad said into his mic. "Let him go until he clears people and structures. Then take his ass down."

When the Serb left through the front glass door and turned right on the sidewalk out front, Konrad started to run, pulling his gun as he reached the door and stopped.

"I'm coming out," Konrad said. "What's his status."

But Konrad didn't need an answer to that question. He heard the tires burning and the engine turning, which made him hurry out to the sidewalk, his eyes scanning the tiny piazza out front. But the car must have been parked alongside the side of the building.

Holgar ran up to his partner and said, "We didn't have a chance. There were too many people. The car must have been waiting for him down that side street."

Konrad said, "Tell me you have eyes on our suspect from Geneva."

"You said to let him go."

"The Serb said he had a bomb," Konrad said. "I couldn't tell you to follow the guy. But assumed you would have someone do so. Which way did he go?"

Holgar pointed to where the car just took off. "Also that way."

So, the car had picked up both men, Konrad thought. He shoved his gun back in its holster and nearly lost his shit, gritting his teeth with anger. These men must have known they had followed them from day one. He felt like a complete idiot. But now he was determined to catch these bastards.

24

Cosenza, Italy

Jake and Alexandra had dropped off Elisa and Vito in Salerno, where Jake convinced the Italians to give up using a government vehicle, which could be easily tracked. Of course, the same was true of nearly every modern car, assuming those who were looking for them knew which vehicle they were using. In this case, Alexandra had rented the car for them under her Russian persona, Alexandra Bykofsky, using a credit card with only a thousand Euro limit.

Before getting to Salerno, Jake had gotten a call from Kurt Jenkins. The former CIA Director had two things for Jake. First, he had been able to track down the current GPS coordinates of the man that Elisa had tracked from Athens. And second, the specifics on the phone number Jake had gotten from the bartender the night before. Since the man from Athens was in Taranto, in the Apulia Region, and Jake's target was in Cosenza, in the Region of Calabria, they had no choice but to split up.

By now Jake guessed that Elisa and Vito were still on the road to Taranto, since that port city was a lot farther away than Cosenza, which was damn near in Jake's back yard. He was quite familiar with this small city along Autostrada A3, the backbone running down the length of Calabria. The city of 70,000 residents was nestled in the mountains at the confluence of two small rivers. In the northern edge of the city, just off the autostrada in the small community of Rende, was the University of Calabria.

Kurt Jenkins had traced the phone number to a college professor who lived a couple of blocks from the university. With the long drive and the short day, it was nearly dark by the time Jake and Alexandra pulled up to the professor's neighborhood and spotted the housing complex. There sat a cluster of four buildings, each one with four attached apartments.

"What do you think?" Alexandra asked.

"I'm guessing these are professor housing," he said. "Those we passed down the road looked like student dorms. Which one is it?"

"Lower level on the left," she said. "Are you sure he has no family?"

"That's what Kurt said. No family, no roommates. As far as he could tell, no pets."

"What kind of professor is he?"

"Mathematics. He's thirty-two." Jake found a photo he had been sent to his phone, and he showed it to Alexandra.

"He looks a little like Stalin," she said.

"I'm guessing his politics are similar." Jake checked his watch.

"You're wondering about Elisa and Vito?"

"Trying to calculate when they will arrive," he said.

"That has nothing to do with us. They will be simply watching the man from Athens."

During the drive from the Amalfi Coast to Calabria, the two of them had had time to discuss how they wanted to play this guy. She had been somewhat reticent to go too aggressive, since the bartender in Positano had not specifically given up the professor as her contact. But Jake had assured her, upon a more detailed review, that the professor was involved—if nothing more than an additional conduit for a larger network. He knew that the best terrorist networks involved layers of isolation and detachment. And this professor, Jake was assured, was up to his eyeballs in crap.

They waited patiently in the car until they saw a man walk up to the first-floor apartment and let himself in, turning lights on like he owned stock in the power company.

"Let's go," Jake said.

The two of them used Alexandra at the door. A man was much more likely to open the door for a pretty woman than a brusque-looking, dangerous man. Of course, this professor had no idea just how dangerous Alexandra could be.

After a quiet knock on the front door, the professor opened the door and was surprised to see a gorgeous woman at his place. But Alexandra didn't say a word. She simply pulled her gun, which she had held behind her back, and shoved it into the professor's face. The man backpedaled into his living room.

Now Jake rushed in after the two of them. "Sedersi," Jake said, telling the man to sit down.

The man hesitated, so Jake snapped a backfist into the man's sternum, taking his breath away and knocking him back into the leather sofa. The professor struggled for air. While the man gasped, Jake hurried through the house finding the man's cell phone and laptop. Searching deeper, he found four additional phones— each with a number on it from one to four. Burners, Jake thought. Perfect. He found a small satchel and shoved everything into it before heading back into the living room, where Alexandra sat across from the professor with her gun pointing in his general direction.

She asked Jake in German if he had found anything. The professor's eyes brightened, so Jake guessed he understood German.

"The normal shit," Jake said in English, with a German accent.

The professor obviously understood English as well. Jake took a chair close to the professor and bore his intense gaze through the man. But he held back from saying anything yet. What had Jake learned so far? The professor had posters for artwork, and the theme of those were quite obvious. The man was a devout anarchist with Marxist-Leninist tendencies. He also had photos framed of various protests, where the professor was prominently featured.

"You understand English," Jake said.

"Of course," the professor said.

"Good. This will be much easier for me. Not so much for you, though."

"Is this a robbery?" the Italian asked.

"Not exactly. You are going away for a very long time. Your only choice is whether you are in a pine box or a prison cell. It's entirely up to you. You must decide now. I will give you thirty seconds to decide."

The professor shifted his stare nervously from Jake to Alexandra and then back to Jake. "You are kidding, of course."

Alexandra took this. "He does not joke." Her English was always accented with German, so now their intonation matched. When the time came for the professor to describe who had interrogated him, he would swear to God it was a couple of Germans.

"What do you want to know?" the Italian professor asked.

It wouldn't come this easily, Jake knew. Not once the man knew what Jake was seeking. Without saying anything, Jake got up and went to the man's bathroom. Jake had noticed that the man was meticulously manicured, so he would use that against him. In one of the drawers he found a small kit, which included a number of instruments—from clippers to tiny scissors to cuticle implements. That would work. Before closing the drawer, he saw a small sewing kit. He grabbed that as well and went back to the living room.

"What do you want?" the professor asked again. This time much louder.

Jake shifted his head to Alexandra, who pulled out a device from her jacket pocket. They had used this with the bartender the other night to keep the screaming down, and it had worked great. Saved on having to find a remote location for the interrogation. It was essentially a rubber ball attached to a rubber strap, used most often by a dominatrix. She had bought it for this very purpose recently.

First, Jake zip tied the professor's hands in front. With a more dangerous character he would never do this, but he didn't expect much fight from the anarchist professor. Then he bound the man's ankles with another one. Once the man was appropriately subdued, Alexandra shoved the ball into the professor's mouth and wrapped it around the guy's head.

Jake started to ask questions. Of course, there was no way for the man to answer, so Jake stuck to yes or no questions for now. His questions were carefully worded as usual. The last thing an interrogated wanted to do was give away what he already knew. Jake would let the man tell him these things. Eventually, Jake got to a point where he wanted to know some new information. He dug into the small backpack and pulled out the laptop, opening it onto the coffee table. But it was password protected.

"Password," Jake said.

The man shook his head.

Jake opened the little manicure kit and looked for something to use. Then he saw the sewing kit and decided to start there. He pulled out a long needle with a short piece of string attached. Jake smiled and then moved over to the sofa and sat next to the professor, who started to look quite concerned.

Grabbing the man's hands, Jake took the needle and slowly started to shove it up through the finger nail of the professor's left index finger. The man tried to scream in pain, but the ball in his mouth kept him from making anything more than a gurgling sound, which brought spittle out from the sides of the ball. Sweat immediately bubbled up on the man's forehead and above his lip. Jake got ready to pierce the middle finger, but the man shook his head vehemently.

"You have something to say?" Jake asked.

Nod, nod, nod.

"Okay." Jake looked at Alexandra, who slid the man's laptop in front of her.

Pulling the ball out slightly, the professor told her the password for his computer. Jake shoved the ball back into place.

"See, it's much better if you tell me what I need to know before the pain. Because eventually you will tell me everything I want to know. Do you understand?"

Nod, nod, nod.

"Good. Now we have a plan." Jake glanced at Alexandra, who gave him a thumbs up.

She would navigate through the laptop quickly. Having worked for German Intelligence for more than 20 years, she knew her way around a dirtbag's computer.

Jake picked up the bag of phones he had found in the bedroom—one smart phone and four numbered burners. First, he checked the man's main cell phone, which was not password secured. Checking the call log, he saw just one call to the bartender in Positano. Okay, that call had been a mistake, Jake guessed. He should have used one of the burner phones. Next, he turned on all of the disposable phones. These were password protected.

Glancing at the professor, Jake asked for the pin for phone number one. He pulled the ball out of the professor's mouth.

"They will kill me," the professor said.

"What do you think I might do to you?"

"You are with the government," he said. "You must follow the law."

Shoving the ball back in the man's mouth, Jake shook his head and smiled. "You're a mathematician. So you know the saying about assuming certain factors in an equation. Well, you have grossly misinterpreted who I am and what I will or will not do—especially to a Marxist professor."

Jake played with a couple more fingers until the man nearly passed out with pain. It was also possible the man was close to pissing his pants, or shitting himself. That would change Jake's calculus.

But the man gave Jake the pin numbers for all four of the disposable phones. The pins were only different by the last digit, which corresponded with the number on the phone.

Now came the hard part, Jake knew. He would need to associate each phone with a contact—the name, number and location—along with any other information the professor had on the contact.

Once Jake got onto the first disposable phone, he saw a possible problem. There was only one phone number that the professor had called on the phone. But he had received images attached to texts from that same phone. He looked at the images and tried to discern their meaning. All of the images depicted scenes of graffiti. As he went over the next phone, the same was true. This one had the number of the bartender from Positano, and Jake realized that the woman had made a mistake when she accidentally called the professor from Cosenza on the man's normal cell phone. The bartender had also sent images of graffiti. Guessing he would find the same on the others, he simply packed them into the bag.

Now Jake had a fresh line of questioning. What could the professor tell them about the graffiti? This might take more than needles in the fingers, Jake thought. Even more importantly, who did this professor report to? There was no way that this professor was running everything from his humble home in Cosenza.

25

Taranto, Italy

Night had settled across this extreme southern city on the Ionian Coast, the smoke and smog from factories reflecting the city lights into the appearance of a massive jazz bar in a smelly cellar.

That's how Elisa Murici always considered this working port, which was founded by the Spartans in 706 B.C. The city had always been an important port for commerce and the Italian Navy, but that did nothing for its aesthetics. If Naples was the rectum of Italy, then Taranto was the sphincter that allowed the crap to flow freely.

Elisa sat behind the wheel of their rental car, a VW Passat, her eyes on an apartment building in a cluster of squalor between the main train station and dilapidated warehouses along the port.

"Do you think your man from Athens is still in the apartment?" Vito asked from the passenger seat.

"I don't know," she said. "We don't have a current reading on his GPS."

Vito glanced at his cell phone, which he had been viewing all night. "Shouldn't we have an app for that?"

They should have an agency with some balls, she thought. It was as if they didn't want to catch these terrorists.

"Put that damn phone away," Elisa said. "Let's go get this bastard."

"We have no authority," he reminded her.

True. But could they afford to wait for more evidence against the man? They already knew the man had worked as a bomb builder in Iraq years ago. "Nobody comes to Taranto for the scenery," she said.

Vito glanced up the street. "It's not such a bad city. If you like rats and garbage."

"Let's go," she said, opening her door.

Once out on the sidewalk, a crumbled concrete with weeds breaking through the cracks, they walked slowly toward the apartment building.

"What's the plan?" Vito asked quietly.

"Knock and ask for someone else. Assess from there."

The streets were bare, the darkness shrouding the apartment complex in obscurity. She didn't like this. Especially since she wasn't sure she could fully trust her partner.

Just as they were about to head into the building, a red Fiat Panda came up the street and pulled to the curb. Elisa grabbed Vito and pulled him in for a passionate kiss, her eyes checking out the car over her associate's shoulder. She turned the kiss into a hug as someone came from the building carrying a bag.

She turned and took Vito's hand, leading him back to their car. The car took off and then she picked up her pace getting into their car and cranking over the engine.

"Was that him?" Vito asked as he buckled himself in.

"Yes." She hit the gas and rushed after the car.

By now the car was four or five blocks ahead of them. Luckily the traffic in this area was sparse. But that also made tailing them difficult. She needed backup.

"What now?" Vito asked.

She took out her phone, punched in the four-digit code, and hit a speed dial she had programmed in recently. This time her call wasn't routed somewhere strange.

Jake picked up on the third ring. "Yeah. You get the guy?"

"Not exactly," she said. "Just as we were about to go pick up the guy, he bolts from his building and is picked up out front."

"Did he see you?" Jake asked.

"I don't think so. But I need your help tracking the man by GPS."

"Did he have his backpack with him?"

"Yes. I think he's on the move."

"Based on the sound," Jake said. "I'm guessing you're tailing the man."

"That's right."

"Which way is he heading?"

"They are getting onto the autostrada heading west right now," she said.

"That's in our direction," Jake said. "Lay back some and I'll get our people to keep track of him. I'll make sure they've got him on the move to confirm what you're seeing."

"How did it go with you tonight?" she asked.

Hesitation. Finally, Jake said, "We need to talk in person. But first let me make a call and confirm for you. I'll get back to you pronto."

"Thanks," she said. The line went blank. She put her phone back in her pocket and found her way onto the autostrada, picking up speed as she flipped through the gears.

"How's your boyfriend?" Vito asked. "After our kiss, I thought you might have given up on the American."

She refused to engage in such nonsense. "His friend will confirm our guy is on the move."

The car seemed to be picking up speed, and Elisa wondered how the car could even go that fast. The Fiat Panda was not known for its speed.

Soon they had passed out of the western edge of the city and were moving toward the south. Elisa knew that this autostrada ran the entire southern coast into Calabria and ended at Reggio di Calabria before continuing across the Straits of Messina in Sicily.

Fifteen minutes later, as they continued on E90, Elisa's phone buzzed and she picked up without looking at the caller.

"Hello, Jake," she said.

"This is Jake's old friend," a man said.

Instinctively, she sat up in her chair a little. She was now talking with the former Director of the CIA, Kurt Jenkins.

"Yes, sir," she said. "I was expecting to hear from Jake."

"I can give you real-time intel," Jenkins said. "Your man is on the move, traveling at about a hundred and twenty kilometers per hour, approximately nineteen kilometers west southwest of Taranto. Does that sound about right?"

"Yes," she said. "We're about a kilometer behind him."

"Is there anything else you need?" Jenkins asked.

"No, sir. We will stick with the man and see where he goes. Thank you for your help."

"Always willing to help the Italians. Especially one of Jake's friends." The former CIA director hung up.

She glanced at her phone, shook her head, and put it back in her pocket.

"Who was that?" Vito asked.

"The former director of the CIA."

"No, seriously."

"I am serious," she said.

Vito gave a little whistle. "I guess your friend Jake has friends in high places."

"You could say that. Back in the day, the former director used to work for Jake."

"And he confirmed our guy is on the move?"

"Yes." But she wished she knew where in the hell the Iraqi was going. This could be a long drive.

26

Rome, Italy

Derrick Konrad had gotten lucky. A CCTV camera on the side street had caught the license plate of the car that picked up the Serb and the man he had followed from Geneva. Although he could not identify the driver in the video, he could definitely make out the Serb in the front passenger seat. Konrad quickly put out a bulletin on the car, and the license plate had been read going through a toll ticket station on Autostrada A13, heading toward Bologna.

Traveling in an unmarked Polizia car, Konrad and Holgar had the luxury of hitting the lights when needed, allowing them to catch up with the Serb and the man they had tracked from Geneva. But still, Konrad knew he had no choice. If he got the chance, he needed to simply take the Serb into custody. At least that was the plan that he had agreed to with his boss in Switzerland.

Now, they were on the outer ring of the Italian capital, and it was closing in on midnight. Somehow they had been able to stay far enough back so as not to alert the suspect of their presence. Hubris, Konrad guessed. The Serb had thought he had gotten away clean, so they had not changed cars between Padua and Rome.

"They're getting off the autobahn," Holgar said.

"I know. We'll need help once they hit the narrow streets of Rome."

Holgar took that as his cue to make the call. The two of them had been in contact with INTERPOL officers from Rome, who had coordinated help with the local Polizia and Carabinieri. Together, they could monitor the car ahead with a series of other unmarked law enforcement vehicles.

"On the way," Holgar said, just as they were getting off the autostrada. "I have the radio channel set."

Where in the hell were these men going?

Konrad followed, keeping back far enough to remain unnoticed by those in the car ahead. Soon they got help by the Italian law enforcement, who coordinated their efforts centrally. Eventually the car wound through a seedy enclave of Rome, an area of government apartments that housed the poor and the newly arrived to Italy.

Then the subject vehicle pulled to the curb and dropped off the Serb and their potential bomb maker from Geneva.

Konrad parked a block away with another vehicle directly in front of him for cover. "Get on the radio and have the Polizia follow that car," Konrad demanded.

Holgar did as he was told and they watched as one of the unmarked Polizia cars followed the driver.

"Now what?" Holgar asked.

"We have two choices. We sit and wait, or we take them now."

"If the Serb actually has explosives in that backpack, we could be in trouble."

His young friend had a good point. In fact, for all they knew, their man from Geneva could have been carrying C-4 or Semtex all along. When they raided the apartment in Geneva, they had found bomb-making materials but without the actual explosives.

"That's a big building," Konrad said. "We don't know which unit. Have the Italians track down who lives there. And tell them not to only consider those with Arab names. They could be staying with an Italian or another Serb."

"Got it."

If the Italians saw this as merely a law enforcement engagement, they would insist on taking over. On the other hand, if they thought it was potential terrorism, one of their federal intelligence agencies would take the lead. He glanced at his hands on the steering wheel and saw that they were trembling. Konrad built up a bunch of spittle in his mouth, found one of his pills, and swallowed it quickly. It was too soon, he knew, but stress often brought on the unthinkable.

"Are you all right, Derrick?" Holgar asked.

During their time staking out the apartment in Geneva, Konrad had told his young partner about his affliction. He had a right to know, just in case he ended up flopping around on the floor. But Konrad was getting concerned. The onset of his symptoms seemed to be coming much more frequently. He wasn't sure why, though.

"I'm fine," Konrad said. "Just trying to figure out how to best play this."

"The Italians might not give us much choice."

"I know. We are in country at their pleasure. But if we move fast. . ."

"We can ask for forgiveness," Holgar said.

Their radio squawked and someone came across with very fast Italian. Besides German, Konrad was fluent in French and English. But his Italian wasn't great. Especially if he didn't know the subject.

"Could you have them switch to English?" Konrad asked.

"Shit. He said they were bringing in a tactical team."

"When?"

"Pronto. He said they would be switching to another channel and cutting all cell signals."

Konrad pulled out his phone and considered who he might call on such short notice to have the Italians hold off. "They know this man might have explosives?"

"Yes. That's why they want to move fast."

He couldn't really blame them. This was their country. Plus, the Serb was under an INTERPOL Red Notice already. That was enough cause to pick the man up.

"How do they know which unit?" Konrad asked.

"They linked the car that dropped them off to an apartment," Holgar explained.

Within a half hour, Konrad first noticed movement in his rearview mirror. It was a team of heavily armed SWAT members, probably Carabinieri, moving methodically and swiftly up the edge of the sidewalk. All of them wore face masks. Then, looking forward, he saw that the road was quickly blocked off. Looking out his side mirror, he saw the road close off behind them as well. They were good, he thought.

Konrad checked his cell phone and saw that there was no signal now. That was standard procedure, but especially important considering the bomb making materials they had recovered in Geneva, which included cell phone detonators.

SWAT entered the building, and they could hear that another set of units were around the back covering any possible escape.

The two of them listened intently at the radio traffic, trying to discern what was happening.

"What are they saying?" Konrad asked.

"Ready to breech."

Konrad glanced at the building, hoping like hell it wouldn't suddenly explode. He startled slightly when he saw a flash from a third-floor window. Flash bang, he thought.

More Italian.

"They've got them," Holgar said.

Wanting to get out, Konrad stopped himself. The Italians didn't know him. They might consider him a threat. But they didn't have to wait long.

A plainclothes officer finally came up to the passenger side of their car and Konrad lowered the window. The officer identified himself as a primo capitano with the Carabinieri. They spoke English.

Konrad quickly identified himself and Holgar and then asked, "How many were taken?"

"The Serb with the Red Notice, a man with a Swiss passport, and an Italian. The resident of the apartment. His brother also lives there. He was the one who drove the men here. We picked him up about two kilometers from here. Thank you for your help. We will need everything you have on this situation, especially the man from your country."

"I would like to be part of the interrogation," Konrad said, choosing his words carefully. He knew the Carabinieri, like other elite units, could be very paternal with their investigations.

The Italian handed his card across Holgar to Konrad. "This is where we will take the men. It will take time for our forensics team to complete their search of the apartment, but our interrogation will commence within the hour. I've informed our people behind us to let you through the barricade."

Konrad thanked the man and started his engine. Then he pulled a U-turn and slowly drove through the gauntlet of vehicles.

"Could you map their location?" Konrad asked, handing the card to Holgar.

"You got it. Looks like it will be a long night. Any chance of stopping for a quick Panini sandwich or a pizza? I'm starving."

They hadn't eaten since earlier in the day. Perhaps that was why he was shaking. Yeah, they could eat. "Something quick. I don't want to miss out on this interrogation. As soon as we get cell service, call our boss and brief him."

27

Cosenza, Italy

It was a couple of hours after midnight when Malavita capo Sergio Russo knocked on the professor's door and Jake answered. Jake had called the man away from his duties in Naples, needing a place to stash the professor. He guessed Russo would have a place in his home region of Calabria.

Russo stepped into the living room and saw the professor laying on his side on the sofa. "Is he dead?"

Jake came over and said, "Not yet. I think he's given us everything he knows. I need to spend the night assessing a few things, but I need this guy to disappear. For a while."

"So, not for good," Russo said with a smirk.

Alexandra came in from the bathroom. "I thought I recognized your voice. How was the drive?"

"Good and fast. Of course, it helps when you have a special relationship with the Polizia."

She gave the capo a hug, which surprised Jake. She usually didn't warm up to people that fast.

Russo shifted his gaze from the general area of Alexandra's substantial breasts back to Jake. "You want me to babysit this guy for a while? Maybe check one more time to see if he knows anything?"

"Not here," Jake said. "I thought maybe you might have a place here in Calabria to store him until we break down this whole network."

Shrugging, Russo said, "No problem. I know a place. But I've done enough babysitting. That's a job below my position. I think you need to take me along with you. After all, that was the deal."

Jake agreed nonverbally. Then he said, "What do you know about Crotone?"

"It's a nice enough town. Why?"

"That's our next stop." The professor had given up a name and location after a lengthy period of persuasion.

Jake knew that torture rarely worked to extract good information, without proper preparation. The one on the receiving end would say he was a space alien to make the pain stop. The fear of pain was better. Even more important was the fear of what Jake might do to the man's DNA ancestry. Luckily, Jake had found evidence of nieces and nephews from Padua and Venice. Nothing like the threat of hurting innocent children to open the mouth.

Jake wandered through the professor's house making sure everything looked exactly as he wanted, projecting a kidnapping and robbery—at least for a while. Within the next few days, like the others the Mafia held, they would turn the men over to Italian authorities. But not until they had the evidence the Italians would take too long to acquire.

Once the place was right, Jake and Russo carried the small professor outside and placed him in Russo's trunk. They planned to meet in a few hours at a hotel in Lamezia Terme. Jake guessed all three of them needed some rest. Interrogations were hard work.

The Malavita capo drove off.

"Any chance you could drive?" Jake asked, dangling the keys. "I need to make a couple of calls."

"No problem," she said, grasping the keys from Jake. "You did most of the work in there. I just sat around looking like a badass."

"Did you see Russo checking out your tits?"

"Italians love big ones."

They got in and Alexandra adjusted the seat to her height.

"They're not as nice since the baby," she said. "Good thing I'm not still breast feeding. I felt like such a cow."

"What are you talking about? You're back to your pre-pregnancy fighting weight."

She cranked over the engine. "No, I mean I literally felt like a cow, producing all that milk."

Alexandra pulled away from the curb and started out toward Autostrada A3. Driving at a reasonable pace, they could make the 60 or so kilometers in a little over 35 minutes. Jake knew of a hotel at Lamezia Terme, just outside of the international airport. Part of him considered driving all the way to Tropea, but that would take too long, especially since they needed to cut across to the Ionian Sea side of Calabria in the morning.

As soon as they hit the autostrada, Jake called Kurt Jenkins for an update on where Elisa Murici and her partner where at this time.

Kurt answered with, "What did you get?"

"Wow. How about a little foreplay before you ram it home?"

"I know how little you like chit chat," Kurt said.

Jake explained what he had found out from the professor, including the cell phones with the photos of graffiti.

"Can you send me copies of all that data?"

"Sure thing. We're heading toward a hotel now."

"You can send them as an email," Kurt said.

"That's the plan. We'll be there in about a half hour."

"If my math is right, it's after zero two hundred there. An old man like you needs to get some sleep."

"Is that what you're doing now in retirement, Kurt?"

"What's that?"

"Working on your standup routine?"

"Who the hell says I'm in retirement? I seem to be doing more intelligence work after leaving the Agency."

"That's because you're back in the trenches again," Jake said. "You got a little soft at the top?"

"That's what she said." Kurt gave a little drum and cymbal sound.

Jake almost hung up. "Time to go."

"Hang on. Did you say something about Crotone?"

"Yeah, why?"

"That's the stopping point where we have both your friend from Italian Intel and the person she was following."

"Wait. Both?"

"Well, we talked, so I accessed her GPS as well."

"Good idea," Jake said. "They might have just stopped for the evening. Could you text me the coordinates for both?"

"They're on the way. Anything else?"

"Yeah. Could you let me know if either moves?"

"Will do."

Jake got off and checked out their progress on the autostrada. Then he stared at his phone.

"Everything all right?" Alexandra asked.

"I think so. I need to call Elisa, but it's late."

"We're up."

Good point.

Just as he started typing in her number, he got a text from Kurt with the coordinates of both Elisa and her subject from Athens.

Before calling, Jake checked on the GPS locations for both of them. It looked like they were staying at the same hotel, just off the autostrada.

A groggy Elisa picked up on the second ring. "What can I do for the King of Norway?" she asked.

"What?"

"That's what came up when you called this time."

"Oh. Right. Anyway, sorry to wake you from your sleep at that hotel in Crotone, but I have some information for you."

"Same here," she said. "But I was going to wait until morning." She hesitated and continued, "Sorry. It's been a long day. What do you have?"

Jake explained his 'conversation' with the professor from Cosenza, and how they had the man on ice for now. He also told her about the phones, the graffiti and the contact numbers, which were being tracked down as they spoke.

"Graffiti?" she asked.

"I know it's ubiquitous now in Italy," Jake said. "So, I'm not sure we can run down any leads based solely on the images."

"What about codes imbedded in the images?"

"We'll look into that as well. But we really need to get your people in Rome to track down these numbers."

"You're assuming they're in Rome. They could be anywhere in Italy."

"I know. But if I wanted to strike Italy and make an impact, Rome is the Holy Grail."

"You're right. Now, what I have for you. My colleague, Vito, got a call about an hour ago that they picked up a man in Rome. Four men, actually. Two Italians, a Serb with an INTERPOL Red Notice, and a Middle Eastern man traveling under a Swiss passport."

Sounded like the start of a bad 'man walks into a bar' joke. "How are they related to our efforts?" Jake asked.

"We don't know. We were tipped off by a Swiss INTERPOL officer who tracked the man from Geneva. They were investigating a potential terrorist cell there, raided the apartment, and this guy got away. They recovered a lot of bomb making materials in Geneva. At the time, the INTERPOL thought they were planning an attack on either one of the international organizations in Geneva, or the banking industry in Zurich."

"Good work on his part," Jake said. "What's the Serb wanted on?"

"A long list of crimes dating back to the Balkan War," she said. "The International Court wants first stab at him."

Jake wished he could get his hands on the guy. He had done some work in the Balkans during the war there and was part of a team that discovered mass graves. "He's the explosives guy," Jake surmised.

"Why do you say that?"

"It makes sense. I'm guessing he was a former officer in the Serbian Army."

"That's right. I can send you info on the man if you want."

"Not necessary," Jake said. "We have to move on the professor in Crotone tomorrow."

"You think he's the top of the food chain?" she asked.

"More than likely. My contacts are running a background on the guy right now. We'll know more in a few hours. You're staying in the same hotel as the man you followed from Athens?"

"I had to get close enough to verify his identity," she said in her own defense. "Besides, until you just told me, I assumed the man was just stopping here for the night on his way somewhere else."

"But now you have to guess he's there to meet with the professor."

"Makes sense."

Yeah, it did, Jake thought. "We're staying in Lamezia Terme tonight. Then we'll drive to Crotone and meet you. Let me know if the man you've tracked from Athens starts to move."

"I will. We were able to place a tracker on his car before going to bed. Now we won't have to depend on your Agency for GPS tracking."

"Nice. Do you have eyes on his room?"

"Vito is on shift now. I was sleeping."

"I get it. Carry on."

"See you tomorrow."

Jake hung up and put his phone back in his pocket.

Alexandra glanced at Jake. "So, how's your girlfriend?"

Should he come clean about his brief relationship with the Italian intel officer? To what end? He explained what Elisa had told him.

"This is a meeting with the professor," Alexandra said. "Just before they put their plan into action."

"I was thinking the same thing. But now we have a pressing concern."

She shifted her eyes at Jake, uncertain.

Jake continued, "Now that their terror network has been broken up slightly, they're much more likely to strike sooner."

Alexandra tightened her grip on the steering wheel and let out a heavy breath. "We need to move fast."

He couldn't disagree with that. But they also had to make the right moves.

28

Lamezia Terme, Italy

Before going to sleep the night before, Jake had compiled all the data he had gotten from the burner cell phones, sending everything to Kurt Jenkins, who had turned everything over to the Agency. This case was getting too big for Jake to handle on his own with just a few assets. He needed all hands on deck in Rome, while he and his friends tracked down the Crotone professor.

Jake woke to his phone buzzing on the hotel nightstand. Still in a sleepy daze, he picked up without seeing who was calling. "Yeah."

"Jake? This is your favorite pilot."

He sat up in bed and then realized Alexandra was taking a shower. His favorite pilot was former Air Force General John Bradford, who was the current CIA director.

"Shit must be getting real if you're calling," Jake said.

"You could say that," Bradford said. "As you mentioned to Kurt, we did check on the potential embedding of data within the images. And we found a simple series of numbers in each."

"GPS coordinates," Jake provided.

"Right. You really should consider coming back to work for us officially. You could be collecting a pension by now."

Jake laughed. "I've made enough in the private sector to retire three times from your organization."

"I've heard your current benefactor pays quite well."

"Maybe you should retire and get on the gravy train."

"I'll consider that."

Jake hoped the DCI stayed right where he was, though. He needed a friend in high places.

"What about the phones themselves?" Jake asked.

"The Italians are working on that," the director said. "I'm not sure if you've heard, but they took down a cell late last night."

"The one with the Italians, the Serb and the Swiss Arab?" Jake asked.

"You are still dialed in, Jake. The Serb isn't talking. The man from Geneva has also said very little. But the Italians seems more helpful. They're spouting off all kinds of radical non-religious dogma."

"Such as?"

"Anarchist crap littered with Marxist strands."

Jake thought back on his interrogation of the Cosenza professor last night. He too was mostly concerned about total anarchy. He even had posters of famous Marxists throughout history. He told the Director about his interrogation.

"Interesting," Bradford said. "But finding a professor with Marxist leanings is like finding a fish that can swim."

The shower stopped and Jake glanced at the door to the bathroom momentarily.

"Right," Jake said. "But what if this is more? What if the anarchy movement has finally gotten organized and is teaming up with radical Islamic terrorists?"

"Organized anarchists? Now that would be a first. It kind of defeats their entire purpose. They're all about destruction of the status quo. Chaos theory."

Alexandra walked out of the bathroom entirely naked and almost said something, but she stopped when she saw Jake on the phone.

"I should get going," Jake said, his eyes on his naked girlfriend.

She sat on the bed next to Jake and reached her hand under the covers, taking hold of his rising interest.

"One more thing," Bradford said. "We looked into that professor from Crotone."

"Yeah," Jake said, as Alexandra pulled his full erection from his underwear and started to stroke it.

"Officially the man is on emeritus status following a series of incidents at his university there."

Jake nearly choked, but not as much as Alexandra, who had taken his erection into her mouth and was working it expertly. "What kind of incidents?"

"Spewing all kinds of radical ideas from Anarchy to Marxism. Normal things for liberal arts professors, but this guy was teaching advanced mathematics and physics."

"Not exactly appropriate in any circumstance," Jake said. "Hard to imagine."

Alexandra came up for air and smiled around his hard shaft.

"They might have been able to overlook some of his issues, but then he started to say he was the reincarnation of Pythagoras."

"Who was from Crotone," Jake said. "More like Pythagornuts."

Bradford laughed. "I'll have to remember that one."

She was really working him over now and he thought he might explode.

"Are you all right, Jake? It sounds like you're in the bath."

"I'm fine." But he was more than fine as he released himself into her mouth. He waited until he was done before adding, "Is there anything else?"

"Yeah," Bradford said. "Say hi to Alexandra. And maybe send a picture of that new baby."

"Roger that."

They both hung up and Jake shook his head.

"Was that your girlfriend?" Alexandra asked, sitting up in bed now.

"That was the current director of the CIA."

Alexandra turned completely red with embarrassment. "I'm so sorry. I thought. . ."

"I'm not complaining," he said, and then explained what was going on, from the cell taken down in Rome to the background on the professor from Crotone.

"Okay," she said. "I guess we better get going. Have you heard from Russo?"

Jake checked his watch and realized it was nearly ten in the morning. Checkout was in an hour. He got up from the bed and pulled up his underwear. "I'm guessing he's on his way. I also haven't heard from Elisa in Crotone."

"How long for you to recover?" she asked, laying back and putting her right hand to her vagina. "I realize now that I took things too far."

There was no need to recover initially. He simply crawled into her and reciprocated orally until she begged him for more. Just as she was about to reach her climax, he pulled his body up and shoved himself into her with one thrust, sending her into a dizzying ecstasy.

A while later they coordinated their hotel check out with the arrival of Sergio Russo, who waited for them in the parking lot. The sky was overcast and threatening to rain.

"How is our professor?" Jake asked Russo.

The Malavita capo leaned against his car and brought a cigarette to bright orange. Before answering, he blew a stream of smoke out of his mouth and it seemed to linger with the cool, moist air. "He's resting."

Was that a euphemism for being dead? Jake didn't want to know. As far as he was concerned, terrorist assholes like that could be strapped with weights and sunk to the bottom of the sea. Many of the jails in Europe were like Club Med. Jake had been imprisoned in real jails in Tunisia and Russia, where squalor and deprivation were defined.

"What's the plan?" Russo asked.

"Who do you know in Crotone?"

Russo shrugged. "We have people all over Calabria."

"Do you trust these people?" Jake asked.

The capo nodded his head. "My cousin runs that crew."

"Good enough. We might need some help there." Then Jake looked at the car Russo leaned against, which was a new Alfa Romeo. "Nice car."

"It's a loaner."

"Stolen," Jake said with a smirk.

"How do you say in English? Collateral for a debt."

"Makes sense. Why don't you leave it here and drive with us. Ours is an actual rental. And I took out the insurance."

Alexandra chimed in. "Which doesn't matter, since he used false credentials for a man that doesn't exist."

Russo pointed his finger at Jake. "I like the way you work, Jake. We might have an opening for you in our organization."

"You can't afford me," Jake said.

The capo flicked his spent cigarette and said, "You'd be surprised."

Jake pulled out the keys. "Let's go."

29

Crotone, Italy

Elisa had finished her final watch at zero five hundred, before going back to sleep in her room. She didn't wake until a little after ten, when her partner texted her and said their man was down in the restaurant eating a long breakfast. She wasn't exactly pissed, since Vito was supposed to let her sleep for only a couple of hours, but she was a little disturbed that the man had not followed her orders.

She showered quickly without washing her hair, got dressed and gathered her stuff into her bag, and checked out. Elisa had a feeling this guy would be on the move soon. Once she checked out and dropped her bag at the car, she went into the restaurant and sat alone, with a view of both her partner and Zamir. Luckily the buffet was still open. She ordered a cappuccino and got a plate of meat, cheeses and some bread. Before eating, she texted her partner to gather his things and check out of his room. She would keep eyes on their man. Besides, she thought, they still had the new tracking device on Zamir's car.

Vito got up and tried his best to not look at her as he departed the large restaurant. But she did notice that Zamir watched Vito leave. Interesting, she thought. Perhaps the man liked men. She kind of thought that might have been the case even back in Athens.

She was able to eat her meal and drink her coffee before her target got up to leave. As the man passed through the restaurant, he didn't even look in Elisa's direction. She texted Vito that Zamir was on the move back to his room.

Elisa finished and then wandered out to the car, where she sat behind the wheel with her phone out. Now she sent a text to Jake Adams, saying the man would be on the move soon.

No answer. She waited. He could be driving already, she thought. A minute later she got a simple OK from Jake.

Vito was the first to come out of the hotel, carrying his bag over his shoulder. He was pretty, she thought.

But too much into himself. He stuck out too much to work surveillance. One needed to blend in better to the background, and that only happened with average appearance. That's why she used minimal makeup and dressed in clothes like the locals.

Her partner threw his bag in the trunk and got in to the front passenger seat. He lowered his sun glasses and checked her out. "You look tired."

"You're an asshole. Never tell a woman that."

"I don't think of you as a woman," he said. "You are my partner."

"Why did you let me sleep so long?"

"You know. You are older and I figured you needed your beauty sleep. Turns out I was right."

She punched him hard in his arm.

"Ouch," he said. "The girl can hit."

"If I thought you had any balls, I would have hit you there."

"That hurts even more than the punch," he said. "If you'd like, I'll show you how much I have."

"If you haven't figured it out by now," she said, "I don't exactly like men."

He pointed at her. "I knew it. There's no way you wouldn't want some of this."

She smiled. "Right. I'll tell you who has been checking out your ass. Zamir. He wants to pound your ass until it bleeds."

Vito turned away. "That's disgusting. You really think he's gay?"

"Oh, yeah. Speaking of which, here he comes."

They watched as the Iraqi from Athens got into the Fiat Panda. Last night, the Iraqi had dropped off the driver at an apartment in the downtown area of Crotone before driving himself to the hotel. Maybe the man would return the car. But Elisa remembered it was a strange thing to do. Why didn't the driver simple drop off Zamir at the hotel before driving to his own apartment? Or, why not just let Zamir stay at his place for the night?

Elisa started her VW Passat and waited for Zamir to pull out. "Do you have the GPS working?" she asked.

Vito's eyes gazed at his cell phone. "Yes, boss."

"Good. I'm going to stay back and follow from a distance. But I'll bet you he doesn't go far."

"What would you like to bet?" Vito smiled.

"A cappuccino," she said. "A good one. Not the autostrada type in a plastic cup."

"Those aren't so bad."

She shook her head and pulled out after the little red Fiat Panda. They wound through the outskirts of Crotone, up the hills away from town. But not very far. She would win this bet. After only a few kilometers, Zamir pulled through an electronic gate and drove into an estate lined with olive and lemon trees.

Elisa parked down the street with a long-distance view of the place. Jake Adams had been right. This was the address for the professor. He had to be in charge, she thought.

As she sat watching the front entrance, the rain started to fall. First it was a light sprinkle. That soon turned into a heavy downpour. She texted Jake, letting him know she was sitting on the professor. Zamir had driven right to the man's estate. A few seconds later and she got a response from Jake saying he was on the way and would be there in a couple of hours, depending on the weather.

•

Antonio Baroni was in front of his large whiteboard considering what to do with a few new variables. Late last night he had gotten word that his man from Geneva had been picked up in Rome, along with the Serb. That meant two of his cells were out of commission, or at least diminished somewhat. Now they had no choice. They had to move up the schedule. The best time to strike would be the holy season. The second best time to strike was any other day. He plotted those factors into his equation and started to see a favorable pattern. This is quite simple, he thought. A squared plus B squared equals C squared. The only potential change he had for Rome was an alternative point to the A variable, depending entirely on circumstances on the ground. He pulled a small device from his pocket and pressed the largest button. Normally this device simply opened a garage door. But he had programmed the toggles inside to Pi, and his assistant had a buzzer with that same code.

Moments later and his assistant came in, closing the door behind him. "Yes, sir."

"Did our man from Athens show up?" the professor asked.

"He just arrived."

"Good. Gather the men. We have to discuss our next move. How fast can we get the protests together?"

His assistant shrugged. "Almost with no notice at all."

Of course, Baroni thought. Most of them had no jobs, no prospects, no futures. Unemployment for young men in southern Italy was nearly seventy-five percent. Their government had deceived them and let them all down. That was the horror of Capitalism. Only a few got rich. The rest were relegated to scrounging for scraps like rats in the ally. Collectivism was the only true form for any just society, where the individual was only as important as the whole group. Governments were an abomination of dictatorial ambition.

"Sunday," the professor said.

"But sir, that will anger the entire Catholic religion in Italy and abroad."

Baroni smiled. "It will have the largest impact."

"I understand. They will blame the Muslims. The recent immigrants."

Shrugging, the professor said, "They have been wanting to strike Rome for years. We will make it happen for them. The bombers will all be from Muslim countries. The explosives will be from Balkan Muslims."

"What about the Serb they picked up in Rome?"

"He was just one of our contacts. And he will not talk."

"I see."

"Individuals are not important. Others must stand up now and take their place. Gather the men in the courtyard in one hour."

The assistant was about to leave, but he hesitated and asked, "Sir, how will we get word to Rome? Through usual channels?"

"No. Those have been disrupted. Everything will be done in person from now on. We will disburse our people. That's why I sent Zamir back to Taranto yesterday. We couldn't afford to make normal calls."

"That only gives our bomb builders two days."

"They need just one to complete the process," Baroni said. "The devices are already built to the proper specifications. We just need our experts to add the electronic triggers."

"They picked up our man from Geneva," the assistant reminded the professor.

"This is redundancy theory. We still have our man from Athens and one more who is already in place. Two will be enough." The professor checked the large clock on the wall above his main whiteboard. Then he turned back to his assistant, Marco. "Thirty minutes in the courtyard."

His assistant nodded and left.

Antonio Baroni smiled as he glanced at his whiteboard again. How is a government brought down? From within. That is the easiest way. The government had opened the gates to the invading hordes, and now he would make them pay for their stupidity.

30

Jake Adams got to Crotone by late afternoon. They had stopped at a seaside restaurant for a large lunch, not knowing when they would get their next meal.

A light drizzle fell upon the city, the gloom of cloud cover bringing the hillside above the town to near darkness.

Jake pulled up behind a car and got out. He glanced back inside at Alexandra and Russo and said, "Do you know how to get to our meeting place?" he asked Russo.

"Of course," Russo said. "It's not far."

Nodding, Jake quietly closed the door and approached Elisa's car, a dark green VW Passat she had rented after their event on the Amalfi Coast. Elisa got out and closed the door behind her, leaning against the side of the car.

Elisa kissed Jake on both cheeks. "They are still inside."

"No other way out?"

She shook her head. "I walked the perimeter as far as I could, but the estate butts up against the hillside. I guess someone could escape that way. But if we closed off the streets leading in here, they would not be able to go far."

"What about roads above the estate?"

"No. There is nothing there. In theory, one could walk all the way up into Sila National Park from here. There is a road about seven kilometers to the east. But that is through very rough terrain and a number of gorges."

"That's where I would go," Jake said.

"True. But not everyone is as crazy as you, Jake."

He smiled. "I'm glad your sense of humor is intact."

"That's the only thing I seem to have going for me these days."

"You have many fine assets."

Her eyes shifted back to Jake's car, probably concentrating directly on Alexandra. Then she turned back to Jake and said, "How do you want to handle this?"

That was a damn good question. "We could go in there guns blazing. Kill a lot of bad guys. But we'd also probably get no intel. We have to assume this is their command and control. They could be getting desperate, now that we've taken out some of their people."

"That's my concern as well," she said.

"I'm guessing they'll push up their timeline for a strike."

"I agree."

Jake looked around her at her partner in the car. "Has he kept in contact with his people in Rome?"

"I told him not to say anything until we know what we have."

"Shit."

"What?"

"I'm not sure I trust that young punk."

"He's all right. A bit cocky. Probably like you were at his age."

"I was a captain in our Air Force at his age."

She nodded understanding. Then she said, "I'm getting wet."

Now Jake glanced back at Alexandra before turning again to Elisa. "You know I'm with Alexandra."

"No." She hit Jake in the arm. "I mean the rain."

Right. He knew that. "All right. Why don't you come with me? I'll leave Alexandra with your boy toy to watch the estate."

"I don't understand."

"We have a man with the Calabrese Malavita with us," Jake said. "He's been very helpful so far. He has a number of assets we can use here in Crotone."

Elisa thought it over. "Vito won't go for that. He'll insist on bringing in the Polizia or the Carabinieri at the minimum. Or even his people from Rome."

"I don't give a shit what he wants," Jake said. "He responded like a dazed tortoise on the Amalfi Coast during that shooting. He doesn't get a say."

"I understand," she said. "But as you know, our organization doesn't have a mandate to act on Italian soil. His agency is my only cover."

"I have no cover. Your government can kick me out at any time. Or throw my ass in jail."

"I won't let that happen," she said.

"Good to know." Jake turned to his car and waved for Alexandra to come out.

His girlfriend came over and simply stood for a moment.

"I want you to stay here and babysit our AISI officer," Jake said.

"You aren't going in there alone," Alexandra said.

"No. We're going to meet with Russo's men. But we need eyes on this place in case they make a move. Text me if anyone moves."

Alexandra understood with a simple flick of her chin. She took the car keys from Elisa and got into the driver's seat next to the young officer.

Jake went back to his car and got behind the wheel, while Elisa found the seat next to him. They pulled out in Jake's rental Fiat Tipo.

Russo was right. The location of their meeting with the local Mafia was only a couple of kilometers away. It was a large house with a nice view of Crotone below.

The three of them got out and went to the front door of the house. A man in his early thirties opened the door. He was wearing a green soccer jersey with white numbers on the chest. He was number one. But he had a semi-automatic handgun strapped to his right hip and an MP-5 submachine gun slung over his shoulder.

Russo kissed the man on both cheeks before introducing Jake and Elisa. The Malavita capo didn't mention affiliations for either of them. Smart move. Jake had a feeling that these men had nothing to do with the local soccer team, and would have wanted nothing to do with Elisa's agency. Russo's contact, the local leader, was simply referred to as Pepe.

They wandered into the main living area of the house and at least a dozen men sat around the room, some on the floor, and all heavily armed. They also wore green jerseys with white numbers. The men were watching a soccer match on a big screen TV.

Pepe introduced Jake and Elisa without using names, but all deferred considerably to Russo, standing up when he entered the living room.

"Come to the kitchen," Pepe said. "You have to try my wine. It's from my own vineyard."

They all went into the kitchen but could still hear the soccer match and the occasional cheer when someone on their team did something other than run and kick the ball.

The local Mafia leader poured glasses of wine for all four of them. They all agreed that his red wine was great. But Jake checked his watch. They needed to get a plan going now.

"You are in a hurry?" Pepe asked.

"We're a little under the gun," Jake said. "I'd like to be in place by dark."

"Of course," Pepe said. He pulled up an actual map of the city of Crotone and surrounding area, spreading it across the kitchen table. He pointed out the professor's estate, along with any potential escape routes. "My men will set up here and here. They wear the same jerseys so you don't accidentally shoot them."

That got Jake thinking. He found his phone and took a quick picture of the jersey, but not the face, of the Mafia leader. Then he texted that to Alexandra, telling her to show it to the young officer, and to not shoot anyone in these jerseys.

"How many people do you have?" Pepe asked.

"The three of us and two more on site watching the place," Jake said. "A blonde woman and a young Italian man. But they should be remaining in the car."

"What about communications?" Russo asked.

"All of my men have ear pieces," Pepe said. "We will just need to coordinate the channel."

"Good," Russo said. "So, what's the plan?"

Pepe smiled. "I was hoping we would just go in and kill them all. These foreigners are taking over our country. It's hard to find a real Italian in Crotone. They come by the boatload and our government simply opens their arms to these men. First, we should never let the ships touch the Italian shore. And if they do somehow get here, we give them just one thing. Fuel for their boat. Maybe a little food. Then we turn the damn boat around and send it back to the Middle East or Africa."

Jake thought that was a good plan. If they did that enough times, they would stop coming. "It's a big problem in Tropea as well," Jake said.

"He's right," Russo agreed. "Our people there are willing to act to stop this invasion."

"Let's start here," Jake provided.

Both Italians agreed, while Elisa seemed off in her own world. Jake wasn't entirely sure where she stood on the immigrant issue.

Jake continued, "What information do you have on Pythagornuts?"

Elisa laughed now. "Is that what you've come to call him?"

"Seemed appropriate," Jake said.

Pepe found another piece of paper a little larger than the map. It was a builder's sketch of the compound.

"How did you get this?" Elisa asked.

The local Mafia man shrugged. "I know a guy. He installed the security system. Well, his men did. They're in the living room right now."

"What they built," Jake said, "they can shut down."

Pepe smiled and nodded his head.

"What about the local Polizia?" Elisa asked.

The two Malavita leaders stepped back and protested. "No, way," Russo said. "Pepe was one of them before I made him a better offer."

"I understand," Elisa said. "What I meant was how do we keep them from responding?"

"They will hold back as long as we tell them," Pepe said. "They know that we know where they live."

"Good enough for me," Jake said. "So, here's what I want to do." He studied the professor's estate and ran his hands through the compound, coming up with details of his plan.

31

Alexandra sat uncomfortably in the driver's seat of the car down the street from the professor's estate. The young AISI officer seemed more interested in his phone than talking with her. She guessed she could whip out her breasts and the man wouldn't even notice. But she needed to know if she could trust the guy.

"Are you updating your social media status?" Alexandra asked Vito.

"Is that what they consider a joke in Germany?"

Now she wanted to punch the little snot in the nose. "You know what your problem is?" She didn't wait for a potential answer. "Your problem is you have no respect for those who have come before you."

This got the young man's attention. He stopped texting and glanced at her. "Alexandra Schecht. Occasionally known as Alexandra Bykofsky. Formerly with German BND, your Foreign Intelligence Service.

Don't ask me to pronounce the German title. Anyway, you retired recently after twenty years of service. Your boyfriend is Jake Adams, a former Air Force Intelligence Officer and CIA officer. But he never seems to retire, because he continues to work for that Agency as a private security consultant. From everything I've read, he was quite good in his day."

"Jake is still quite good," she said. "Do not underestimate a man because of a little gray at the temples. In the spy game, gray means you have been around long enough to not get killed."

"I'll remember that." His eyes now studied her more carefully. "Considering you just had a baby six months ago, you look good."

Okay, now she was seconds away from punching this little punk in the mouth. But she let him stick is foot in his mouth a little deeper. "Continue."

"All right. A couple years ago you bought a nice place near Tropea. I'm guessing it was getting a little too cold in Austria and Germany."

Jake had placed their home in Tropea in a corporate trust, so this AISI officer had really done some digging. "Why do you care about us?"

Vito shrugged. "I like to know who I'm working with."

She didn't want to mention this to the youngster, but Jake had also run down information on him. They knew everything about the man, but there was no reason to let him know that they knew him, from praise to flaws.

"What is your assessment?" she asked.

"Of you and your boyfriend? Or of our current situation here in Crotone?"

"Yes."

"Okay. You and Jake are civilians now. As far as I'm concerned, you have no official reason to be part of this whole investigation."

"That's your problem," Alexandra said. "You consider this an investigation."

"What would you call it?"

"An existential threat caused by an invading force," she explained. "You have opened your castle doors to a marauding horde."

"They are people just like us."

"No. They are different. They don't want your tolerance. That's weakness to them. They want you dead."

Alexandra got a text from Jake with an attached photo of a green soccer jersey with white letters, with Jake explaining that was what their Italian friends would be wearing. Don't shoot!

"Fellow human beings just want to be treated with dignity," Vito espoused.

"Mostly you are correct," she said. "But if you let a thousand through the gates and just one decides to kill, you have a major problem."

"The gates are opening," he said.

"They're wide open," she agreed.

"No, the professor's gates are opening."

She quickly glanced down the street and saw that he was right. Then a car slowly crept out of the gate, turned right and drove off. That car was followed by a second one, which followed the first down the road in the opposite direction of their position.

Damn it, she thought. "How many in those two cars?"

"I couldn't tell."

From that distance, without binoculars, she was not able to catch the license plate numbers. But she put to memory the makes and models of the cars. They were both four-door dark brown Fiats. The new models.

Pulling out her phone she started to text Jake. Then she asked Vito, "Do you have any movement on the man you and Elisa were following?"

"No, the tracker was on an older model red Fiat," he said. "The other device we would have to rely on different sources."

She let Jake know that status, including the type of cars that left the professor's estate.

Jake responded back almost immediately, saying to hold tight. They were on their way.

"What's happening?" Vito asked her.

"I don't know." But she had an idea. "I need to get a closer look at the estate." She unbuckled and started to get out, but Vito grabbed her arm.

"Where are you going?" he asked. "We need to wait for backup."

She twisted his hand off of her arm and got out, leaning back in to say, "Stay here. I'll be right back. The others are on their way." She showed Vito a photo of the soccer jersey and told him not to shoot those wearing the green and white.

"You should wait for help to get here," he pled.

He wasn't concerned, she thought. He was afraid.

Alexandra shook her head and quietly closed the door. Then she drifted toward the sidewalk. By now the low cloud cover had blended with impending darkness to partially obscure the neighborhood in a gloomy haze.

Luckily the rain had stopped, but the moist air brought a chill to her exposed skin.

She stepped lightly down the sidewalk toward the estate, wishing she had done so before the two cars had left the compound. What if those cars held a strike team each? They could be going anywhere in Italy. Or, they could just be going out for pizza.

When she got to the front gate, she slowed her pace so she could look through the metal bars toward the large house. But with the massive olive trees lining the front part of the compound, there was no way to see the house.

Once she passed the gate, she continued along the tall outer wall that lined the large estate. Glancing about the neighborhood, she noticed there was no way for anyone to see her next move. With a swift movement, she climbed the wall and dropped to the other side.

Now she pulled out her gun and moved up a slight rise toward the house in the distance. She half expected to encounter roving patrols with attack dogs, but that didn't happen. Then she had a strange feeling. What if this entire scenario was simply a ruse? What if the man from Athens was simply coming to meet with an old professor? What if those they had interviewed had pointed toward the outspoken professor to draw them away from the real threat?

She moved with as much stealth as possible through the olive grove. Luckily the rain had soaked the ground so the fallen leaves were not crunchy.

In a few moments she came along the edge of the large estate. Out front she could see a few more vehicles, including the red Fiat that Elisa and Vito had placed a tracker on.

Her eyes kept scanning for video cameras and possible motion sensors. But there was nothing along the perimeter that she had been able to see. None within the olive grove either. There. The house itself had a number of cameras. Based on the models she could see, they would probably cover an area at least 50 meters out, and they more than likely included motion sensors.

Now she was stuck behind a large olive tree, wondering what she should do. Jake would have a plan, she thought. She needed to get inside. Needed to show Jake that she still had what it took to be a covert operative.

What if they were right and this professor was running the show? By now he would have gotten word that his people were dropping off the face of the Earth—not responding to his calls. This could force his hand.

Make him push his plan forward quicker. Desperation could make the man do just about anything. She was frozen now, unsure what to do. Her phone buzzed and she pulled it from her pocket, shielding the light from the estate behind her jacket.

It was Jake saying he was on his way. Don't do anything stupid. She texted him, saying she had eyes on the estate house and what she had found for security.

32

Jake had gotten to the estate with Elisa, parking temporarily behind her car and stepping up the sidewalk alongside her car. When he saw that Alexandra wasn't there, he quickly texted her after first confirming with Vito what she was up to.

"I told her to wait for you to return," Vito said to Jake.

"Yeah, well she doesn't listen sometimes," Jake said. "She's used to working alone."

Elisa said, "What about our plan?"

"We stick to it," Jake said, still typing to Alexandra and explaining what would happen. "Let's go."

Russo had taken a position with his Malavita friends down the other side of the road. By now, the estate was cut off from all road traffic.

Elisa explained their plan to Vito. He would hold tight at the car and monitor their activities, backing them up if needed.

Jake and Elisa would make a direct approach on the estate, seeing if the professor would simply let them in based on a ruse. They got into Jake's Fiat Tipo and drove up to the estate entrance, where Jake pressed the security button and smiled for the camera.

A younger man came on the screen and asked what they wanted.

Jake explained that they had some information about a professor from Cosenza and needed to discuss this with Professor Antonio Baroni.

The young man didn't answer, but he did pause for nearly a minute. Then the gate suddenly started to open.

Taking that as a sign to move, Jake drove through the gate and noticed in the rearview mirror that it quickly closed behind him. As he drove up the narrow curving road through the tall olive trees, he wondered where Alexandra was at this time. Hopefully, somewhere where she could see them coming.

"What do you think?" Elisa asked.

"I think this professor has quite the ego," Jake said. "Which is why I thought he would open the gate."

"Now that we got in, how do you want to play this? He could just have his people shoot us."

"No. First he'll want to know what we know."

"And then he'll shoot us," she said with a nervous smile.

"Turn on your comm," Jake said. He also turned on his comm and heard Alexandra immediately. "Where are you?"

Alexandra gave her position and asked what to do.

"What's the status of the security system?" Jake asked Russo, without naming him.

"It's cut," Russo said.

"You hear that?" Jake asked Alexandra.

"Got it," she said. "I'll move in closer once you get inside."

Jake pulled up behind a black Audi, blocking it in. Into the comm he said, "One and five move in closer." One was Pepe and five was his main man, along with three others in their teams. They would take up positions on foot along the perimeter of the walls in case someone tried to escape on foot. The remainder of the Malavita crew would stand back at the road blocks with their cars.

He turned to Elisa and said, "Are you ready?"

She nodded and the two of them got out.

The young man who was on the security screen at the gate opened the door and stood with his hand blocking their entry.

"What can I do for you?" the man asked in Italian.

Elisa took this one. "We must speak with Professor Baroni about an old friend of his from Cosenza."

The young man seemed to undress Elisa with his eyes. Without saying a word, the man waved them in and closed the door behind them. Jake spoke German lightly into his comm, saying the front door was unlocked.

The man turned and said, "Scusi?"

Jake shook his head.

They continued through the mansion, which was quite elaborate. But Jake already knew what to expect. He had found some photos online of the inside of the house from just before the professor purchased the house five years ago. What they were not able to find out was how a man with a professor's salary could afford such a large estate. Jake could see that the professor had made some improvements in the past five years, including the security system. But also the frescos on the ceilings of some rooms. The place looked more like a Venetian palace than a Calabrian country house. This guy had money from somewhere.

The younger man let them into a double door, which put them in a modified library, with large whiteboards taking up most of the space. The man closed the door behind them, leaving Jake and Elisa alone with the professor.

Jake glanced at the mathematical scribbling on the whiteboard and had flashbacks to his college math classes. Not happy memories. He had no idea what the professor was doing with these equations.

The professor stood with his back to them. He wore a full blue suit with light gray pinstripes. He was taller and more fit than Jake would have guessed, based on his thick, short silver hair.

Baroni turned and shifted his eyes from Jake to Elisa as he stroked a long sterling goatee, cropped to perfection. The professor would have looked distinguished were it not for his simian features. He spoke to them in Italian, discussing innocuous things like the terrible weather and the state of politics in Europe. Jake stuck with Italian for now, trying not to give up any more information than he needed to at this time—not even their names.

"Your Italian is quite good, Mister. . ." Baroni said in German.

Jake said nothing.

Baroni continued, "I hear a hint of a German accent in your Italian. But your Italian is also littered with Calabrese dialect." He turned to Elisa, who had said only a few words, and he said in Italian, "You are from Rome." He hesitated, as if trying to assess them, but he was clearly having a difficult time trying to understand who they were and what they might want. "A German who speaks nearly flawless Italian, and a beautiful Italian woman," the professor said, switching to English. "Both of you look like you could snap a man's neck with your bare hands. Especially you, sir. You are an impressive figure."

"No shit," came a voice in his ear. Alexandra on his comm.

Jake gave him one of those looks like he might just show the man how a neck snaps in real life. But he said nothing. Not yet. He liked to give a man just enough rope to hang himself.

"My assistant mentioned something about a professor from Cosenza," Baroni said. He left it like that.

The two of them had decided to let Jake do the talking, since Elisa would have to eventually bring this man in for potential prosecution. She didn't want to worry about giving rights to the guy.

"You know who I'm talking about, Baroni," Jake said, a particular edge to his words.

Now the Italian professor looked confused again. "American English. Now that's interesting. But you're not law enforcement like the FBI."

Jake said nothing.

The professor continued, "Maybe CIA. You have that whole mysterious spy type quality to you. You're a thinker like me."

"I'm nothing like you," Jake said.

Baroni shifted his attention to Elisa. "You also look like a spy of some kind. Italian External Intelligence and Security Agency?" He paused for a reaction. "That can't be, though. Since you are not authorized to work within Italy."

Jake broke in. "Your English isn't bad. You must have learned from watching exclusively gay TV."

The professor laughed. "You think my lisp is from sucking cock? But I assure you, I like women. You are wasting my time."

"Then tell me about your big whiteboard," Jake said. Something clicked in his mind about the math. He had been told that the man likened himself to a reincarnation of Pythagoras. There was a geometric symmetry to the man's calculations. Layers of triangles intersected at various points, like a three-dimensional graphic of some kind. Then there were various sections of calculations off of each angle.

The professor's eyes shifted slightly, but his head didn't turn away from Jake or Elisa. "You would not understand."

"Because you're Pythagornuts?" Jake asked.

The professor laughed and then said, "You have an interesting disposition." He twirled his fingers as he added, "One part smartass indifference; one part resident badass."

Time to bring it on home, Jake thought. "Can we cut through the bullshit? I don't give a flying fuck what your whiteboard says."

This prompted Elisa to take a quick series of photos of the man's work with her cell phone. Just in case the man decided to erase everything.

"Sent," Elisa said with a smirk.

Jake continued, "We have you running a terrorist network throughout Italy. All we need to know from you is how you want this to end. My guess is that you know you are beat, so you decided to put your plan in motion sooner rather than wait for the Holy season."

The professor's complexion turned ashen as he shoved his right hand into his pocket, and Jake wondered if his pocket was big enough to hold a gun. Definitely not. But he could have an explosive trigger, Jake guessed.

"You know nothing," the professor said. He produced a small electronic device and showed it to Jake. "You see this? It's a simple object with three buttons—each with its own purpose."

Jake shook his head. "We know that two cars with men just left your compound. We're guessing you've decided to send them instead of using your old communication devices, with disposable cell phones and coded photos of graffiti."

Professor Baroni reacted with shock this time. He couldn't hide it.

"I know. Every good plan can be defeated," Jake said. "We're going to take you in now."

Recovering now, the professor said, "Do you think I would let myself be exposed like this without a significant force protecting me?"

"Maybe you don't have a choice," Jake said. "We have already collected your intermediaries. We are rounding up your cells in Rome as we speak." This was possibly a little lie. Jake had no idea how long it would take the Italian authorities to react with his intel.

"I have the Malavita on my side," Professor Baroni said.

Elisa shot Jake a quick glance. Had the local Mafia double-crossed them?

"That's bullshit," Russo said over the comm.

"Nice try," Jake said. "I don't believe you."

"Why is that so far-fetched?" the professor asked.

"First of all," Jake said, "the local boys despise this invasion of their country by foreigners. And second, they're on our side."

The sound of gunfire broke the silence, and both Jake and Elisa drew their weapons.

33

As Jake and Elisa went in the front door of the estate, Alexandra observed shadows of men coming from the back of the building, one particularly close to her position. So close, in fact, that she could not speak into her comm unit.

She wasn't sure who fired the first shot, but she thought it had to be somewhere out near the front of the estate. Perhaps even over the wall on the street.

Fast Italian came over her comm ear piece. Although she was relatively fluent in the language, she was having a hard time understanding this garbled yelling.

By now, the man roving the area near her was almost upon her position. And she had made one error. She had not given herself an easy retreat. At least not without being seen by this man.

She glanced at her hand with the gun and saw that it shook slightly. Then her mind reeled back to her baby girl at her home on the Calabrian coast. Emma should have been the last thing on her mind right now. Push it back, Alexandra.

The man stepped closer, now within just a few feet.

More gunfire at the perimeter of the estate, which startled the man with the gun.

She was pinned down here. Shifting her body slightly, she snapped a twig beneath her right foot.

The man stopped and cast his gaze and his submachine gun toward her.

With one motion, she dove and shot three times. The man reacted by firing off a long burst from his rifle, the bullets spraying the olive tree in front of Alexandra and flying over her position. But her three shots had hit their mark, dropping the man into a bundle in the wet soil.

She rolled over and got to a crouched position, her eyes shifting toward the front of the house. The shooting had alerted another man, who ran toward her location.

Alexandra got up and ran around the side of the house toward the back door. As she rounded a corner, she came face to face with another man, who startled before reacting. She was quicker, shooting the man once in the chest and once in the face. Then she shoved her body against the corner of the house, knowing she was being chased.

With a quick look around the corner, she saw one man, who had his gun pointed toward her from the other end of the building. But she was able to scoot back around the edge just as the first bullets hit the building near her head.

Think, Alexandra. If they sent someone around the other side of the building, she would be pinned down in the crossfire—a sitting duck. She didn't wait for that to happen. Instead, she swiftly pointed around the corner and shot three times. Then, immediately after her shots, she ran toward the back of the house, entering the unlocked door.

Inside now, out of breath, she said into her comm, "Coming in the back door."

•

When the first gunshots went off, Jake's mind immediately thought about Alexandra and that she must have been discovered out in the perimeter. But the shots were coming from too many areas, and some of them seemed to be coming from beyond the estate.

Then Jake heard the Italian over his comm, where Russo and his main lieutenant Pepe directed his men. They were under attack. At first they had no idea who they were shooting at, but then it became more clear to Russo. The gunfire was coming from two sources—from the perimeter wall on one side, and from behind them down the block. The Polizia. Russo had obviously miscalculated the response of the local police.

Based on the smile on Professor Baroni's smug face, Jake guessed that the man had alerted the local Polizia as soon as Jake and Elisa had gotten to the front gate. Baroni must have said that his estate was under attack by some unknown force. If the professor had said it was the Malavita, they might not have responded.

Elisa was at the door with her gun, waiting for Jake to make a move. "What now?" she asked.

"Our friends are under attack," Jake said. Then he pointed his Glock at the professor's head. "Tell your men to stand down."

"Why should I?" the professor asked. "This is private property and we are just trying to protect ourselves from some rogue agents and Malavita thugs."

Jake noticed that the man had put the electronic device back in his pocket. Obviously the professor had sent his men to attack with a simple signal from that remote control.

Moving closer to the professor, Jake switched his gun to his left hand. Then with one quick snap of his right hand, he struck the professor in the nose, breaking it and sending blood flowing everywhere.

Baroni staggered backwards, both hands covering his nose and the man screaming in pain.

Jake sent a quick front kick, catching the professor in the nuts and dropping him to his knees. At that very moment, with gunfire having just come from outside the side of the house, he heard Alexandra say over the comm that she was coming in the back door.

Twisting to his side, Jake snapped a kick into the head of the professor, sending him careening backwards and knocking over a smaller whiteboard.

"We need him alive," Elisa said.

"Then you need to subdue him," Jake said. "I'm heading out."

Elisa nodded as she put her gun back into its holster under her arm. She dragged the professor from under the whiteboard, shoved him back to ground onto his face, and shoved her knee into the man's lower back. Then she pulled a long zip tie from one of her coat pockets and lashed the professor's hands behind his back. With the man tied like a hog, Elisa gave Jake a thumbs up.

Jake nodded and went to the door. Before going out, he hesitated. Then with one fluid motion, he opened the door, his gun leading his way, and rushed out.

Gunshots immediately traced his path, slamming first against the door and then along the wall, until Jake could scoot behind one of the thick marble columns. It was the professor's young assistant shooting from near the front door.

Now against a marble column, Jake tried to keep his body from the constant gunfire. The young man had a submachine gun and Jake just had his Glock. He was definitely at a disadvantage.

Suddenly, from behind Jake, came a salvo of gunfire. He turned and saw Alexandra at the end of the long corridor, crouched against the right side.

The gunfire stopped, but smoke and the smell of powder filled the air.

"Can you see him?" Jake said into his comm.

"He might have gone outside when I shot," Alexandra responded.

Jake waved her forward while he kept his gun trained toward the front of the house.

She got up to him and nudged her body against his. "What's going on? I lost my comm for a while."

He told her Elisa was behind the double doors holding onto Professor Baroni. Then he said, "What's going on outside? It sounds like a war zone."

"It is. What now?"

"Now we get the professor out of here. Russo and his friends are shooting it up with the local Polizia and the professor's men."

She nodded agreement. "What about the rest of the house?"

"I'm guessing we got what we need," Jake said. He stepped out from behind the column and nobody shot at him, so he guessed the guy had gone out the front door.

Jake went to the double doors leading to the professor's office, and slowly opened it. Elisa was on the other end pointing her gun at Jake. She quickly lowered her weapon once she realized it was Jake.

"Let's get that asshole out of here," Jake said.

By now the professor had recovered from his little nap and was sitting up dejected, his nose almost twice the size of normal. Jake and Elisa lifted the man to his feet.

"Did you check him for weapons?" Jake asked.

Elisa showed him the clicker. She had already removed the battery. "Just this."

They hauled the man outside to their car, with Alexandra and Elisa covering Jake while he manhandled the professor. Jake thought he had blocked the Audi in front of their car, but someone the driver had simply ran over a large shrub and gone around through the wet grass. Probably the same man who had just been shooting at Jake.

Gunfire continued at two corners of the property, where the Malavita had set up their road blocks.

Jake shoved the professor into the back seat. Alexandra got back there on one side of him, while Elisa took a position on the other side.

Getting behind the wheel, Jake started the car and backed around far enough to make a turn toward the front gate. Then he slowly started to drive down the road, his eyes open for any trouble.

Into his comm, Jake said, "On our way out in the Fiat Tipo."

"It's still hot out here," came a man's voice. It was Russo.

"Understand. Polizia?"

"They backed off once they realized it was us. Now it's just the men from the compound. Do we need any to live?"

"No. They're all collateral. Fire away."

"You got that shit right," Russo said.

Seconds later, the gunfire intensified on both sides. When Jake got to the gate, it failed to open.

"Hang on, people," Jake said.

He gunned the engine and dropped the clutch. The car lurched forward and he hit the gate just as he punched it into second gear. The gate buckled and burst out into the street. Jake twisted the wheel to the left as he hit the road, the tires squealing against the pavement.

Then Jake hit the brakes and the clutch simultaneously, bringing the car to a halt. Looking ahead, he could see and hear gunfire. Behind him, looking in the rearview mirror, he also saw flashes of gunfire down the road.

He turned back to Elisa and asked, "Where is your partner?"

She looked confused. "He was supposed to monitor our communications and stay with the car."

Jake looked ahead again and saw that the VW Passat that Elisa and Vito had driven to Crotone was not where they had left it. Without looking back, Jake said, "Try to get him on the phone. See where the hell he went."

While she checked her phone, Jake pulled out his phone and called Kurt Jenkins.

"Yeah," Kurt said.

"Could you track that GPS from the man?"

"The one from Athens?"

"Yep."

"Give me a minute."

As Jake waited, he glanced back at Elisa. "Anything?"

Elisa shook her head. "And I tracked his phone. It says it's just up the road about fifty meters."

Jake let out the clutch and drove slowly up the road until he got to the spot where they had left Vito in the car. He put the car in neutral, pulled up the hand brake, and got out. The young AISI officer's phone sat in a small grassy spot alongside the sidewalk. Next to that was Vito's communications ear piece. Jake picked both up and turned back to their car, showing Elisa he had found the phone.

Kurt Jenkins came back on the line. "Jake. We got the GPS moving about sixty-five miles an hour to the southwest by Catanzaro."

Damn it. That meant the Iraqi bomb builder from Athens had to have left in one of those two cars just before they moved in on the compound. Jake asked Kurt to keep track of the car. They had Professor Baroni, and would bring him to Rome.

"Are the Italians ready to take out the cells in Rome?" Jake asked.

Kurt cleared his throat. "They're hesitating. But they have all of the locations under surveillance."

"You tell them that the strikes will happen soon." Jake glanced back at the professor in their car. "I'll find out when. But if I had to guess, I would say Sunday."

"Shit."

"Yeah. I better get going. We need to get to Rome."

34

Jake turned the driving duties over to Alexandra, so he could continue to work the phone with Kurt Jenkins. He also placed Elisa in the front passenger seat and told her not to observe what he was doing in the back seat with Professor Baroni.

The car with the bomber had about an hour head start on them, so they were pushing it hard to catch up. But that time difference also gave Jake some time to have a frank discussion with Pythagornuts.

"So," Jake said, "Let me get this straight. You use Pythagoras and his theorem to justify your actions?"

The professor predictably huffed at Jake's oversimplification, shaking his head vehemently. "No, no, no. Pythagoras himself was a brilliant man. He could see patterns in everyday life that could be explained by mathematics and physics. Some believe that he must have been a time traveler, sent to his time to forward society. Perhaps all of the great thinkers were similarly placed—from Copernicus to Galileo to Di Vinci. It was no coincidence these people came to Italy."

"Copernicus was Polish," Jake said. "And technically Pythagoras was a Greek. Same with Archimedes."

"Copernicus was born in modern-day Poland, but his first language was German. The city in Silesia where he was born was Germanic, or more specifically Prussian. But that's not important to my thesis."

"What is important?" Jake asked. He needed to let the professor talk his way into his own funeral. Jake could tell the man had narcissistic tendencies.

Professor Baroni explained his own theory in great detail, until Jake's eyes glazed over or until his bullshit meter spiked. Then Jake would redirect the conversation. This went on for hundreds of kilometers. Jake was building a rapport, trying his best to understand the man. The conclusion? The man wasn't exactly Pythagornuts like Jake thought. The professor was a true believer that anarchy was the only way to destroy the corrupt governments of Europe. Then they could start anew, building a new society based on Marx and Engels. Turns out the professor was more of a Friedrich Engels fan than a follower of Karl Marx.

Finally, Jake said, "Okay, I think I understand. But tell me one society that has benefited from Communism or Marxism?"

The professor shook his head and rolled his eyes. "I see. You're one of those Capitalist purists who thinks that all of society's ills can be cured by striving for money."

Okay, now Jake had the guy right where he wanted him. "Well, money hasn't cured cancer."

Baroni laughed. "We could have cured cancer decades ago. But the big pharmaceutical companies make too much money off of those afflictions to allow a cure to reach the people."

Jake slapped the seat in front of him near Alexandra's shoulder. "See, that's what I've been saying for years. Those bastards in power would rather have millions of people die from prolonged painful deaths just so they can make money."

"Are you mocking me?" the professor asked.

"Hell no. I'm pissed. My parents both died from cancer." A total lie. But it fit Jake's current narrative.

"I'm sorry," Baroni said. "We have all lost too many people."

Time to move in for the kill. "Why do you think we don't work for the government?"

Baroni looked confused. "But you are all agents of the government."

Jake shook his head. "Not even close. Do you really think we're bringing you for prosecution?"

The professor's eyes shifted with uncertainty. "Yes?"

"No. We work for a loosely formed group of altruistic philanthropists. I know that's kind of redundant. But that's how they think of themselves. Anyway, they are concerned with the governments of Europe also. But mostly they are worried about innocent people. They're like the Catholic church without all the pedophilia."

"That's an overblown generalization," Baroni said.

"I agree. But that's my point. You see, if you blow up a bunch of historical sites in Rome who do you hurt?"

The professor said, "The government of Italy."

"To some extent, yes," Jake said. "But really you hurt the people of the world. Those people who come to Rome to see the ancient civilized world. You also hurt the little shop keeper selling goods to tourists. You hurt the baristas and pizza makers." He pushed forward, thinking he might have the professor turning toward him. "Also, by doing so, you taint another religion."

"The Muslims do this to themselves by not cleaning their own house," Professor Baroni protested.

"True. But by striking on Sunday in Rome, you could start a religious war."

"We need a revolution in this world. The meek are the anarchists. And they shall inherit the Earth."

"Matthew is important," Jake said. "But so is Peter." Of course, Jake was fishing for St. Peter's Square as a potential target.

The professor said nothing.

"You have not denied that you plan to strike Rome on Sunday," Jake said. "We know this to be true."

Baroni licked his dry lips, his tongue touching the caked blood that had flowed from his broken nose. "If you don't work for the government, then why do you care what happens in Rome. Just stay away."

Perfect. "We have a better plan. It's easy to send young suicide bombers out into a crowd of people and blow themselves up. You just guarantee them a bunch of virgins upon their death, along with martyrdom. They're easily swayed. So, since you're so willing to let others do your dirty work, we thought we might give you an opportunity to participate in the action. I won't say you'll get a bunch of virgins, but you don't want them anyway. Most virgins are that way for a reason. They're probably ugly and nobody wants to have sex with them. I could offer you a dozen or so hot porn stars willing to do anything. Admit it. That's a deal."

"You're crazy," Baroni said. "I will not participate."

"You won't have a choice. Are you all right? You seem to be a little thirsty."

"I could use a drink," the professor said.

Jake leaned forward and said, "Isn't there some water up there?"

Elisa reached under the front seat and produced a bottle, opening it and handing it back to Jake.

With the professor's hands bound, he couldn't drink on his own. So Jake helped the man. The professor sucked down most of the water and sat relieved.

By now they were on the outskirts of Naples, but Mount Vesuvius was in the way from seeing most of the lights, since they drove around the back side of that famous mountain.

Jake watched as the professor quickly drifted off.

"How much sedative did you use?" Jake asked Elisa.

"Enough to knock out a horse," she said. "He'll be out for hours."

"Cool." Jake got on his phone and first called Kurt Jenkins, telling him that the professor had tacitly confirmed the strike would happen on Sunday. Kurt also explained that Jake was now only about twenty kilometers behind the Iraqi from Athens. Then Jake made a call he had been putting off for some time—to his benefactor, billionaire Carlos Gomez.

The Spaniard answered with a groggy greeting. "It's the middle of the night, Jake."

"I'm sorry, Carlos. But terrorists never sleep." Jake explained what had happened in the past few days, right up to their current condition.

"You've been busy," Carlos said.

"You could say that. Do you have any sway with the Italian government?"

"Of course. I have many business dealings in Italy."

"Could you get them to strike the locations and pick up these assholes."

"I'll do what I can," Carlos said. "By the way, I have friends with INTERPOL. One of their men from Switzerland followed a potential bomber from Geneva to Rome. Eventually they hauled the man in, along with a Serb."

"We heard about that," Jake said. "What about him?"

"You should meet him in Rome. He might have more information for you. His name is Derrick Konrad."

Gomez sent Jake the man's number and the hotel where he was staying, along with a photo of the Swiss man.

Jake thanked the man and tapped off his call.

"Everything all right?" Alexandra asked, her eyes in the rearview mirror.

"Yeah. Carlos wants us to meet an INTERPOL guy in Rome. He might have some insight for us."

"What about Kurt?" Alexandra asked. "Where's our Iraqi dirtbag?"

"Twenty kilometers ahead. We should catch him before Rome."

Alexandra hit the gas, increasing their speed. It wasn't like they needed to catch the guy before Rome, but they needed to track him once he got there.

Jake pulled out his phone again and considered texting Kurt Jenkins to look into the background of the INTERPOL officer, Derrick Konrad. But Kurt was busy with other things. So instead, he texted an old friend in France to vet the man. He liked to know the people he planned on working with, especially under these circumstances. Considering it was the middle of the night, he guessed that help might take a while.

Finally, he leaned back in his seat and closed his eyes, trying to get a little rest before Rome. The sound of the road blended with the light snoring by the professor. Jake thought about the young AISI officer, Vito Galati, who was still missing. Had he been taken? Or did he simply abandon his post when the shooting began? Time would tell. Elisa had put a search out for their rental VW Passat, but they had not traced the GPS for the car yet.

35

Jake woke to the feeling of his phone buzzing in his pocket. In the darkness he wasn't sure where he was momentarily. He had been dreaming of being trapped in a building with a black apparition floating above him, and he was helpless to respond. When he tried to yell, his throat seemed to collapse and no words came out—as if a demon had taken control of his body.

His heart raced out of control and he took in deep breaths of air. Then he remembered his phone and he checked on the caller. It was Kurt Jenkins saying the car had turned off the main autostrada west of Rome. He glanced about, seeing that Elisa was also asleep in the front passenger seat.

"Where are we?" Jake asked Alexandra.

"On the outskirts of Rome. I was about to wake you for an update."

"The car turned to the west toward Fiumicino Airport."

"That's just four kilometers ahead," she said.

Elisa stirred and woke, wiping her mouth with her sleeve. "We're in Rome."

"The car is heading toward Leonardo Di Vinci," Jake said.

"There were two cars," Elisa reminded them.

"I know," Jake said. "But we have no idea if they're still traveling together."

Jake made a quick call to Kurt Jenkins, who answered on the second ring.

"You're close now," Kurt said. "Looks like they're heading toward the international airport. Could that be their target?"

"It's possible," Jake said. "But I have a feeling they want a bigger impact than that. The professor was coordinating a number of cells. Each one was headed up by a local Italian. An anarchist. But I believe, based on those we killed in Crotone, that the majority of the terrorists are from Muslim countries."

"Do you have word on the status from Crotone?" Kurt asked.

Jake leaned forward, tapping Elisa on the shoulder. "Any update on Crotone?"

Elisa checked her phone. "I'm sorry. I missed these texts coming in." She read through her texts and said, "The local authorities moved in once the shootout stopped between the Malavita and Baroni's men. They've taken just a couple of men into custody. All of those taken in and dead hold Middle Eastern passports."

Getting back on his phone, Jake said, "Did you hear that?"

"Yes," Kurt said. "Thanks. I'll pass that along."

"Any word on your partner?" Jake asked Elisa.

She shook her head.

In the phone, Jake asked, "Where are they now?"

"Instead of going to the airport, they turned south into what appears to be a residential neighborhood."

"South of Fiumicino Airport?" Jake asked.

Kurt directed them on which road to take. Jake passed this on to Alexandra.

"That's Isola Sacra," Elisa said. "Lido del Faro. The Tiber River splits off a canal a few kilometers up stream, making the area an island of sorts. It's mostly working class people living there. Airport workers."

"The car has stopped," Kurt said into Jake's phone. Then he said the address, which Jake relayed to Elisa, who put it into her phone GPS.

Jake checked his watch and guessed the sun would be up in about two hours.

"Thanks for the help," Jake said. "We'll take these guys down."

"Are you sure you don't want to wait for backup?"

"From who?"

"Right. Good point. The Italians are still sitting on the other locations you gave them."

"And the Agency? Are they being brought in on this?"

Hesitation from Kurt. "We think so. The Italians know you have the professor. They got the photos sent from their officer showing the man's mathematics, which they don't understand."

"That's because the professor is nuts," Jake said. "But somehow he has learned how to herd cats, coordinating the efforts of radical Italian anarchists and Muslim extremist terrorists. This is a deadly combination. If the Italians won't act, I will."

"There are too many cells, Jake."

"Perhaps. But my guess is they have destroyed all of their communications devices. Now everything will be done by personal messenger." Of course, he thought. That's what was going on with the two cars. These were messengers.

Jake leaned forward and asked Elisa to show the location on her electronic map for the cells they had identified. All of them were more in the downtown area, close to soft targets. Ancient Roman cites.

"All right," Jake said, into the phone but also to the two women in the front seat. "We will find only one car from Crotone here."

Elisa turned to Jake. "How do you know that?"

"Because one car had personal couriers with orders from Baroni," Jake said. "And the one we're following is something else. Based on the man you followed from Athens. The Iraqi bomb builder."

"Zamir," Elisa said.

"Right. That dirtbag. He will be setting the trigger mechanisms. Probably at this location on the lido."

"That makes sense," Elisa said. "Then they can combine the triggers with the main explosives sometime today and ready them for use tomorrow."

"That's right. We forced them to move up their schedule. We can't let this Zamir escape."

"Which way?" Alexandra said, coming to a street light.

"Sorry," Elisa said. "Turn right. Then it's three blocks and turn right again."

Alexandra did as she was told. The streets were nearly empty at this hour.

"What do we do with the professor?" Alexandra asked.

Kurt spoke in the phone to Jake. "Turn him over to our Agency folks."

"That won't go over great," Jake said to Kurt.

"What?" Alexandra glanced at Jake in the rearview mirror.

"We'll shove him in the trunk. How much longer will he be out?"

Elisa turned and smiled. "I'd guess four to six more hours."

"Guys," Alexandra said, slowing the car. "That's the Fiat Tipo ahead. Two blocks. Just like our car. Even the same color."

"Pull over," Jake said. Into the phone he said, "Gotta go."

"Be safe," Kurt said.

Then they both hung up.

Here the streets were dark, without street lights. It was a residential area with mostly single-story houses. Jake knew that they didn't have a lot of time to surveil the house where the car sat. If the bomber simply grabbed his triggers and took off, they might lose the man—especially if he decided to leave his backpack behind. Just in case, Jake had an idea.

Elisa had pulled the tracker from the old red Fiat Panda at the professor's house, so Jake got that from her.

"What's the plan?" Alexandra asked.

"Just in case. I need to place this on the Fiat Tipo. Zamir could leave his backpack behind and then we'd have no way to track the guy."

"We'll gag this guy in case he wakes up," Elisa said. "And shove him in the trunk."

Jake got out and flipped down his seat. "Shove him through here in case the neighbors are up and nosey."

Then Jake wandered down the street toward the Fiat Tipo. He would casually place the magnetic tracker under the back bumper and then continue on, making sure to check out the surrounding area.

As he got closer, he could see lights on in the single-story house. Then a dark figure slipped past a curtain and Jake couldn't help thinking about the unsettling dream he had just experienced. Continuing on, he stopped briefly and stooped down to tie his left shoe. While he did so, he swiftly placed the tracker before getting up and strolling down the sidewalk. To anyone watching, it would look like Jake was heading toward the sea for a morning run.

Once he had passed the house, he had two choices. He could turn around and walk back to the car, or he could sit on the place for a while to see what was going down. But there was no good vantage point out on the street. Most of the yard in front of the house was covered by a tall hedgerow, the deciduous leaves still hanging on strong to the branches.

He stopped and glanced back toward their car, seeing that Elisa and Alexandra were done stuffing the professor into the trunk and were heading up the sidewalk toward him.

Just then the front house door opened and a man headed out to the street. Jake was stuck. So he walked toward the Fiat, getting to the car at the same time as the man from the house.

Somehow, the man was spooked and started to run back toward the house. Jake ran after him, tackling the man and bringing him down in the dewy grass. Wrapping his legs around the man, Jake put the man into a sleeper hold. The smaller man struggled beneath Jake, but every move the man made brought a tighter hold around the man's neck—like a python tightening his grip on a rat. But the man wouldn't give up. When the guy tried to pull a gun from a holster under his arm, Jake twisted hard away from the man. Hearing that familiar snap was surprising and disconcerting. The man went limp in Jake's arms.

Oops.

Jake unwrapped himself and got up. As he did so, Elisa and Alexandra rushed to him, their guns out.

"Is this Zamir?" Jake whispered to Elisa.

She shook her head no.

"Let's go," Jake said, shifting his head toward the house and pulling his gun out.

36

Jake knew that it was not smart moving on a target safe house without proper backup, but he also knew that since leaving the Agency he had rarely had that luxury. He did know that they had one less man to take out now, since he had killed the man in the front yard.

Elisa went around back, while Alexandra took up a position behind Jake as they entered the house, their guns out and comm units on.

"In place," Elisa said in Jake's ear piece.

He moved into a long hallway. Ahead he could see what must have been the kitchen. The two of them passed a dark living room and continued stepping toward the light.

A man appeared, looked shocked, and retreated into another room.

"One target," Jake said, still moving forward.

Suddenly the man came around the corner and opened fire on them. Jake shoved his body against the right wall, returning fire. He could feel Alexandra right behind him.

Without turning his head, Jake said to Alexandra. "Retreat to the living room. See if it comes through the other side to the dining area."

Alexandra tapped Jake on the back and took off. Just as she rounded the corner into the dark living room, the man scooted out again, firing wildly toward Jake.

But Jake was waiting for the man. He fired three times. The first bullet struck the man in the right shoulder, seeming to pull him out from behind the wall more, and the next two rounds struck center mass somewhere, dropping the man to the floor.

Now Jake said, "Second man down. Moving forward." Which he did now with purpose, stepping over the dead body and kicking the guy's gun away.

Once Jake got to the kitchen, lit by a small light above the stove, he moved his gun around the small room, seeing that there was a passageway leading to a back section of the house, which could not be seen from the road. This place was larger than Jake had thought. Where was the back door?

"Status in the back?" Jake asked Elisa.

A figure appeared to his left and Jake trained his gun but held his fire. It was Alexandra, who had made her way from the living room, through the dining room, and back to the other side of the kitchen.

Gunfire from another area. The back door?

Jake repeated his request for status from Elisa.

Finally, Elisa said, "One more down back here."

Nodding his head to Alexandra, she followed Jake toward the back section of the house. Coming to a corner, Jake hesitated. With a quick look, Jake saw a man waiting to shoot. Just as he pulled his head back, a dozen bullets struck the wall behind the corner. This guy had a submachine gun, Jake thought.

Jake's heart raced now, but his mind only registered ringing and his nostrils filled with gun smoke. He tried to remember how many shots he had taken. He was still good.

With one quick move, Jake got to the floor and dove out slightly, his gun aimed down the hallway. His mind registered movement and flashes almost simultaneously. He fired a number of times. The man fell to the floor and

Jake kept on firing until the slide on his Glock locked back to empty.

Pulling himself back to a sitting position, Jake dropped the empty magazine to the floor and shoved a fresh one with 17 rounds into the handle. Releasing the slide, a round slapped into the chamber.

"One more down," Jake said into his comm, and also to Alexandra next to him.

How many more could there be? Two? "Status?" Jake asked into the comm.

"Holding at the back door," Elisa said.

"Still haven't found Athens," Jake said.

"There's a dim light on in the far back room," she reported.

"All right. Moving in."

Jake scooted out around the corner and back again. Nothing. He glanced at Alexandra and tapped his back, meaning to watch his six. She nodded.

Together, Jake and Alexandra moved down the corridor. They were at their most vulnerable now, since they had nowhere to go if someone shot at them now. When they got to the dead man, Jake saw that he had hit the man in the leg, the chest and through his nose.

Alexandra cleared the room where the man had taken up his position. Then she came back behind Jake and the two of them moved toward the last room.

Now Jake saw the back door. Into the comm, Jake said, "Moving to the back door."

"Got you," Elisa said.

Jake looked at Alexandra and whispered, "Swap positions with Elisa."

"Why?"

"She's been on this guy since Athens."

Alexandra did as he said, moving out the door and letting Elisa inside.

The Italian intelligence officer mouthed the word 'thanks.'

The last door was on the far right side of the corridor. Jake moved up and listened, keeping back from the door.

Just then came the sound of breaking glass. Jake checked the door handle. It was locked.

Gunfire from outside the house.

Jake shifted his body to the wall across from the door and shoved his foot into it next to the handle. The door gave way and Jake dove to the ground, his gun aimed up.

A salvo of bullets peppered the air, striking the walls and the door opening. But Jake had no shot.

More gunfire.

Then came four or five shots from behind and above Jake. A man fell to the floor, his head hitting the tile surface and his lifeless eyes staring right at Jake from across the room.

Elisa stepped over Jake and cleared the rest of the room.

Getting to his feet, Jake said into the comm, "Status outside?"

"One down out the window," Alexandra said.

But he could see that for himself, since the man was hanging halfway out the window. "Clear in here," Jake said.

Elisa moved about the room and checked the pulse on the man she had shot.

"Is that your man from Athens?" Jake asked.

"Yes. That's Zamir."

Jake glanced about the room and couldn't believe what he was seeing. There were tables with magnified lights and scores of electronics. Not only were there trigger devices used to set off larger explosives, there was a large cache of C4. There was also the beginning of what looked like suicide vests. This Zamir had already completed his first device, which was sitting on a table by itself in a completed area. Jake checked to make sure the device wasn't set to explode.

"Is that what I think it is?" Elisa asked.

Looking over the bomb precursor, Jake found the right wires leading to an electronic device—an older half disassembled cell phone. This was a crude device without a booby-trapped failsafe. Carefully, Jake removed the wires to the phone. Then he slipped the charge from the C4 and set that aside.

Alexandra joined them in the room and gave a little whistle. "Wow. This is crazy."

Elisa pulled out her phone and took a number of photos. Jake did the same thing. Both sent the photos to their people—Elisa to the Italian External Intelligence and Security Agency and her current boss with AISI, and Jake to Kurt Jenkins.

Finally, sirens started to get closer.

Jake glanced to Elisa and said, "You're gonna have to explain this. But I'm not sure you can explain us."

"Our agency will take over, along with AISI," Elisa said.

"Every law enforcement organization in Italy will want in on this," he assured her.

"I'll control the situation," she said. Elisa got on her phone and followed up her text to AISI, the Italian FBI.

By now a few of the Polizia sirens had settled outside. All they needed now was to run across a number of trigger-happy cops, Jake thought.

"Let them know we're in the back," Jake said. "Mention a shitload of bombs. That will slow them down."

Elisa nodded her head and continued to speak with her superiors. In a few minute, she got off the phone and glanced at Jake and Alexandra. "We're good. They will talk with Polizia dispatch and let them know the good guys are in here."

"What about us?" Alexandra asked.

"I told them I was here with two of my agents," Elisa said. "A man and a woman. That's all."

Jake said, "What about the strike on the other cells?"

Elisa glanced about the room. Finally, she said, "That's expected any moment now. Especially now that we have found the bomb builder."

Jake's phone buzzed and he saw that it was Kurt Jenkins. "Yeah."

"You got them," Kurt said.

"We think so."

"Listen, I told you about the INTERPOL officer from Switzerland. He was dropping his partner off at the airport and I redirected him to your location. He should be there soon."

"What does he want with me?" Jake asked.

"Just talk with the man," Kurt said.

"All right. Now, can you cover us here? I've had to kill a few people and don't want to end up in an Italian jail."

"I'll handle it," Kurt said. "Good work."

Before Jake could answer, the phone cut off. He shoved the phone in his pocket.

"Are we good?" Alexandra asked.

Technically, she would still be covered by German Intelligence, but it might be less complex if the Agency just included her under their umbrella.

"We're covered," Jake said.

The next ten minutes were intense. Luckily, Elisa's bosses made it clear to the responding Polizia and Carabinieri that they were the good guys. Once the police realized that this was an operation above their level, they simply stood back and played crowd control.

Eventually, officers from both AISI, internal security, and Elisa's external intelligence agency, showed up and started to assess the situation. This would be the greatest win for both organizations in a long time. Both Jake and Elisa guessed that they would fight over who got credit for the operation. Jake would make damn sure that Elisa got her due. After all, she had tracked this Zamir all the way from Athens, managing to place a tracking device on the guy.

They had made their way outside just as the sun started poking through the clouds on the horizon.

"How you doing?" Jake asked Elisa, who seemed somewhat despondent.

"You make things interesting, Jake," Elisa said.

Alexandra smiled at the Italian woman.

"If you're persistent enough, good things happen," Jake said.

"Relentless," Alexandra said.

Jake shrugged. "That too."

An officer with the Italian Internal Information and Security Agency came up to the three of them and sheepishly waited for a lull in their conversation. He was a man in his early thirties. Finally, he asked Elisa, "We understand that you have a Professor Antonio Baroni, a suspect in this investigation."

Jake pulled out the keys to his rental car and handed it to the young man. "He's in the dark brown Fiat Tipo down the block. He's tied up in the trunk. If you have a couple of hours to waste, ask the guy about the Pythagorean Theorem."

The man took the keys but looked confused as he walked away.

"Now that's just cruel, Jake," Elisa said. She looked at her watch. "Let's go. We have a front seat to the raid."

37

On scene two blocks away, just inside the police cordon, sat a large command vehicle owned by the Italian Internal Information and Security Agency, although to most outside observers this would appear to be a massive black van.

At precisely 0700, AISI, backed up by special tactical units of the Carabinieri and the Italian Polizia, simultaneously moved in on the positions Jake and his team had discovered.

On large LED screens split in four, they all watched as the tactical teams moved in. On other screens they could toggle through body cameras worn by every member of the teams.

Jake thought about how technology had changed over the years. When he first started with the Agency, they were still using film in cameras. Sure they had some video surveillance, but nothing like they used today.

"You did this," Jake said to Elisa.

Coming out of a daze, Elisa shook her head. "You did this, Jake. I was just along for the ride."

As they watched the raids turn into shootouts, a man came in from the back of the van. Jake studied the man and concluded based on the man's age and attire and the small image sent to his phone, that he was the INTERPOL officer from Switzerland.

The man introduced himself as Derrick Konrad reaching his hand out to Jake.

Shaking the man's hand with a firm grasp, Jake said, "I understand you wanted to talk with me."

"It's the strangest thing, Mister Adams," Konrad said.

Jake held up his hand. "Jake is fine."

"Okay. Anyway, I got a call from my boss in Switzerland, who had gotten a call from his former boss in France. Some old timer retired from INTERPOL, I understand. So, this man knows you. Said you were associated with a former INTERPOL officer from Austria."

Now Jake understood. "Yeah, I know who you're talking about. What does he want?"

"I don't know for sure," Konrad said. "He mentioned something about a friend. I believe a wealthy benefactor, who you happen to be associated with now. But he didn't mention a name. I'm very confused."

"Welcome to the intelligence business," Jake said.

Konrad smiled. "I was able to take a look inside this not so safe house. The devices were similar to those we found in Geneva. My guess is that our man was on his way here, but he knew that we were closing in on him."

"Either that or we didn't catch all of them," Jake said.

Pointing at the screens, Konrad said, "We'll soon find out. It was mentioned to me that the professor from Crotone was planning on using an anarchist protest to lure a bunch of people to the target sites tomorrow."

"That's what we understand," Jake said. "We also found suicide jackets only partially constructed. Our guy would have been working all day to put those together. My guess is that this is not over. There could be more cells. Let's hope the Italians can have some balls with the professor from Crotone."

"This would have been a blood bath," Konrad said.

Jake agreed with a simple nod. Then he turned his attention to the screens again, where a number of flash bangs and shoot outs were taking place. He hoped like hell that these men had not gotten any explosives previously.

Elisa stood and pulled her phone from her pocket, moving away from the screens. She mostly listened, but then said a few words before hanging up. Now she came to Jake.

"What's up?" Jake asked.

"They found Vito Galati," she said.

"Where? At the country club or the video arcade?" Jake quipped.

She shook her head. "He claims that Baroni's assistant took him hostage up in the Sila National Park. He finally escaped this morning."

"Where is he now?"

"Still down in Calabria," Elisa said.

Jake introduced the INTERPOL officer to Elisa, and then explained how she had tracked the Iraqi bomb builder from Athens to Italy, taking him down in the house. He was making damn sure that Elisa got credit for all of this. Jake had no interest in recognition. He never had that desire. Just get the damn job done. That's what mattered.

Moments later, someone declared that all of the strike teams had cleared their locations. A sigh of relief turned into cheers and back slaps.

Jake and Konrad stepped outside and shook hands one more time. "Thanks for stopping by," Jake said. "Is there anything else I can do for you?"

"Perhaps," Konrad said, but he seemed a bit unsure. "I believe I'm being recruited for something. But I'm not sure what that might be."

So that was it, Jake thought. His Spanish billionaire friend, Carlos Gomez, had heard good things about this INTERPOL officer. Now Gomez wanted to add this guy to their team.

"Why do you say that?" Jake asked.

"I'm supposed to meet with a guy in Monaco," Konrad said. "There's a private jet waiting at the airport to take me there. I'm a bit concerned."

Jake smiled. "Are you happy with your job?"

Konrad shrugged. "It can be frustrating."

"I understand. Take the flight. It's a nice plane. Listen to what the man has to say. And maybe we'll work together in the future."

The Swiss man nodded his understanding. He thanked Jake again and wandered back toward the Polizia cordon barrier.

Alexandra nudged up to Jake and said, "Are you ready to head home?"

"I'm tired."

"I drove almost all night," she reminded him.

"Good point. What say we drop off the car at the airport and fly home."

She touched his hand and said, "That's what I was thinking. I'll call my cousin and tell her we're coming home." Alexandra wandered up the street toward their rental car.

Elisa came over to Jake and took this opportunity to give him a big hug, her eyes up the street on Alexandra. Then she pulled away and squeezed Jake's hand. "Thanks, Jake. You really deserve all the credit for this."

"No. I did what I needed to do. You did what they pay you to do."

She came in again and the two of them kissed on each cheek. "I'm still going to make sure my boss understands we did this together."

"What about Vito?" Jake asked.

Shaking her head, Elisa said, "We'll have to see about him."

Jake gave her a parting smile and wandered back to his car.

38

Tropea, Italy

Two days removed from all that had happened in Rome, and Jake and Alexandra had settled back into their life with their young daughter Emma in Calabria. Both of them had done a lot of sleeping in that short while.

It was early evening now and Jake had gone into the city of Tropea with Sergio Russo, their new Malavita friend. Russo had a special contact for one of the specialties of the area—great, fresh seafood. They had just purchased five fresh tuna steaks right at the boat of a fisherman who had caught them that afternoon. It didn't get any fresher than that.

Now, Jake drove their Alfa Romeo home along the winding, narrow road, the sun just dropping below the sea.

"You've got a nice place on the coast, Jake," Russo said. "And you don't have to worry about security. My people will know not to touch the place."

"Good to know," Jake said, as he slowed to make a sharp curve. "I'd hate to have to hurt your people."

Russo laughed. "Good point. I've seen how you and your woman operate. Emma is very beautiful. I would hate to be the young man who comes to date her in about fifteen years."

Jake had thought about that as well. But he figured the young men would have just as much to fear from Alexandra.

"You are lucky to have Alexandra's cousin to help with your daughter," Russo said. "Family is everything."

That's what Jake loved about the Italian people. Russo could be one of the most brutal captains of the Calabrese Malavita, yet still extol the virtues of the family unit. Blood was everything to them.

Jake's phone suddenly chimed, and he knew it wasn't a text or a phone call. This was his security alarm. He slowed the car slightly as he found his phone and checked out the video streaming. His system was set at all times, and he never got false readings. On the screen he saw a number of people moving stealthily toward the house.

"Shit," Jake said.

"What is it?"

Jake handed his phone to Russo and then punched the gas hard. "My house is under attack."

Russo kept watching the video stream while Jake navigated the narrow road. Jake knew he was still ten minutes away from his house.

Punching the phone button on his car, Jake said, "Call Alexandra." His phone linked with the car and made the call. But it went directly to Alexandra's voice mail, which had no message. Only a beep. He cut the call short and took back his phone.

Now he drove even faster, to the point of nearly running off the side of the mountain a few times. As he got to his front gate, it was already open. He powered through and could hear the sound of gunfire.

Russo pulled his gun and looked eager to get out as they rolled up to the house.

More gunfire.

Jake skidded to a halt and shut down the engine. As he got out he said to Russo, "You cover the front and I'll go around back." He knew that Alexandra would go to their safe room just off their master bedroom overlooking the sea.

Russo got out and took a position behind the car.

More gunfire. From two directions.

Jake rushed around the side of his house, his gun ready to take out any targets. As he started to round the back corner, he stopped in his tracks when he saw a man with a submachine gun. Jake scooted back around the corner just as the man opened up and peppered the stone wall with bullets. When the shots stopped, he rounded the corner and opened fire on the man as he was replacing a magazine, dropping the man next to Jake's pool.

Now Jake came to the edge of his large sliding wall of glass that led out to his pool from his living room. He stopped to assess the situation. He had no communications with Alexandra or cousin Monica. Where were they?

Gunshots from the front door. More inside.

Jake took in a deep breath and ran inside, his gun firing constantly as he vectored toward his bedroom. He jumped over an obviously dead cousin Monica, her body bleeding profusely. Others in dark clothing also lay strewn about Jake's house.

As he entered the room, he surprised another man who stood before the safe room and was trying to figure out how to breech the heavy door. But there was no way in. Jake got the drop on this man, shooting him several times until his bloody body dropped to the travertine tile.

More gunshots out front, where Russo had to be engaged with the men.

Jake punched in the cipher code to his safe room and the door opened. Then he quickly closed it behind him. Alexandra lay against the far wall, blood everywhere, and their child crying in her left arm while she pointed the gun in her right arm at Jake.

She was shaking, obviously in shock. Jake took her gun and set it on the floor. Then he assessed her wounds. She had been hit in the stomach and the chest. Another shot hit her leg. Blood pooled around her torso. Her breathing was weak. More blood dripped from her mouth.

"Monica?" Alexandra asked softly.

Jake shook his head. "I'm sorry."

"Who are they?"

"I don't know," Jake said.

From inside this room, Jake could still hear the sound of gunfire. But the room was mostly sound proof, so the shots were muffled. Russo was still engaged with these men. Jake found his phone and called Russo. Somehow, the man had heard the phone, or felt it buzz in his pants.

"Are you all right?" Russo asked.

"Yes. Alexandra is hurt. I need to get her help. Can you make it around the back?"

"Yes," Russo said. "But they've set the house on fire, Jake. The front is fully on fire."

"Meet me by the pool," Jake said, and then clicked off.

He got down with Alexandra, whose eyes were swirling around in their sockets. He knew what that meant.

"Jake," she said, barely audible.

"Yeah."

"Take Emma and get out." She had switched to her native German.

"I can't leave you."

"You must, Jake. I love you. But you must leave me. You can't take me and Emma. I won't make it to the hospital."

Emma continued to cry. It wasn't a full scream, but more of a whimper.

Jake hugged Alexandra and kissed her on the lips, tasting her blood. He knew she was right, but he had a deep-seeded desire to not leave her behind. It was something not of his DNA. When he pulled back to protest, he gazed into her eyes. But the life had gone from her. There was nothing he could do for her now. She was gone. Their life together was gone. And now he would have to take his daughter and also leave.

He pried Emma from Alexandra's lifeless grip and placed her on his lap. Then he found their go bags and took a minute to make sure he had what he needed—including his guns and credentials. He put Alexandra's Glock in his holster under his arm and made sure he had a fresh magazine in his own.

Jake stood, slung the bag over his head and shoulders, and gathered the strength to move forward.

Just as he was about to leave he noticed that the gunfire had subsided. That could be good or bad, he thought.

He opened the safe room door and smoke rushed in. Now he ran through the house, Emma on his left side crying as he found his way through the smoke to the back of the house. Flames crawled up the sides of the walls at a number of locations. He covered Emma's face with his hand as he hurried through the house to fresh air outside.

His lungs were nearly bursting by the time he exited the sliding doors to the patio area by the pool. As he came around the side, Russo met him. The Mafia man lifted his gun and Jake was confused for just a second as the man shot around Jake, taking out another man in black.

"Where's Alexandra and her cousin?" Russo asked.

Jake choked and coughed to try to get rid of the smoke from his lungs. "Gone."

"I'm so sorry, Jake. But we need to go. There are at least five more out front."

He wanted to hand over his baby to Russo and go out front to kill every last one of those bastards, but he knew that the safety of his daughter was paramount now. He couldn't afford to let her get hurt. She was everything to him.

They started to go around the outside of the house, the only side that didn't seem to be on fire, since this was the side with the master bedroom and the safe room. As they got toward the front of the house, Jake looked around the edge, his gun ready to shoot anything or anyone moving.

His Alfa Romeo was fully on fire also. Then it blew up and Emma started to cry again.

Jake turned to Russo. "There's another way out. Follow me."

The two of them ran to the back yard, past the swimming pool, to the edge of the property, which sat on a high cliff overlooking the ocean. But Jake had made a path to the ocean when he first moved in. He glanced up at one of the cameras he had installed to protect this side of his property, and his phone instantly signaled that someone was there. It was still working. So he guessed the others were also working.

They made it down the side of the hill in the darkness toward the rocky beach below. Once they moved far enough away, Jake turned to see his house in full flames, the smoke rising up high to the sky.

Sirens now echoed through the early night, the sound eerie and surreal to Jake. All he could think about was the body of his girlfriend, the mother of his child, being consumed by flames.

Once they got almost to the town of Tropea, Jake stopped and turned to his friend Russo. "You were never there," Jake said. "As far as you know, I'm dead. Do you understand?"

"Of course. What will you do? Where will you go?"

"It's better if you don't know."

Russo nodded agreement. "I understand. But I will find out who attacked you. I promise that."

"Thank you."

"I can get a car in Tropea and drive you anywhere," Russo said.

"No. You should go home. I'll take it from here."

Russo nodded. Then he hugged Jake, kissed Emma on the forehead, and kissed Jake on both cheeks. He wandered up toward the city on a narrow path.

Emma started to fuss again. Jake found a bottle inside the go bag and put it into her mouth, which she immediately started to devour.

Now, like no time in his life, Jake felt alone. Yes, he had Emma. But he had also lost so much. He felt cursed. He had lost three women to violence—two had died in his arms because of his failure to protect them, and the third had died alone. How could he ever allow another woman into his life? How could he protect this little baby from his curse?

Jake wandered into Tropea as he formed a plan on where to go and what to do.

39

Tropea, Italy

Elisa Murici wandered around the perimeter of the Polizia crime scene tape, observing what had been the home of Jake Adams and his girlfriend, Alexandra. She imagined that it must have been rather splendid before it was turned to a pile of charcoal. All of the bodies had been removed from the ash—ten men and two women. The Polizia had responded first, along with the fire department. By then, the shooting had ended and all that remained was the inferno.

The Polizia then turned the investigation over to Italian Internal Information and Security Agency. AISI officers were still trying to decipher what had happened at Jake's place. The only reason Elisa had been allowed on site was because of her mandate to work with Vito Galati of AISI, and the fact that Jake Adams had become a hero to the Italian government. Unofficially, of course. They could never publicly admit that a private citizen had brought down a terrorist network on Italian soil without proper authority. The Italian government was picky that way.

A man appeared from the back of the AISI command vehicle and waved at Elisa to come inside. This single technician had been trying to access the security videos surrounding Jake's seaside house.

"Do you have it?" Elisa asked the young man.

"This man had a very secure system," the technician said. "Everything was uploaded to the cloud. A number of the perimeter cameras are still operational. But the system is private and highly encrypted."

"So, that would be a no, then?" she asked.

"That would have been my initial guess," he said. "But just moments ago I had a file sent to my terminal. A video file from an unknown source."

"What's on it?"

The man swished his head side to side. "I don't know. The file says for your eyes only."

What? How could that be? Elisa tried to understand. How would anyone know that she was even here?

"I'll leave you alone," the technician said, and then left the back of the vehicle.

Before she could access the file, though, she had to type in a password based on a question. It didn't take her long to understand now. She typed in the name 'Archimedes.'

The video started with footage of various men moving toward Jake's house. Then it cut to other cameras inside the house during a horrendous firefight. She gasped when she saw Alexandra with her baby in her arms and blood pouring from wounds on her chest and abdomen. Alexandra dragged one leg as she retreated to another room.

Then another women was seen shooting it out with the men, until she too was shot and killed.

The video switched to another time, showing a man run out the back sliding door and firing. Then, as he changed out a magazine, this man dropped dead to the patio. Next, a man rounded the corner and came inside.

"Jake," she said softly. A tear streaked her face and she wiped it away with the back of her hand.

Now the video switched to the front yard view, where men came into Jake's house with gas cans. Wait.

She backed up the digital file about thirty seconds and let it roll again.

There. She paused the video and couldn't believe her eyes. Shaking her head, anger boiling up throughout her body, she let the video run again.

The last few seconds finally brought a smile to her face. A feeling of elation overwhelmed her as she saw Jake Adams carrying his baby down the back hill toward the sea.

She knew that Jake was alive and had sent her this video for a very specific reason. Elisa got onto the computer system and sent herself a copy of the encrypted file. She pulled out her phone and saw that she had gotten the file. Then she went through and scrubbed the video from that computer system. Even if the technician had saved a copy of the file, there was no way he would be able to crack the password.

She took out her phone and sent a text. Seconds later she got a response. Her meeting was set.

Elisa left the command vehicle and thanked the technician, saying she would have to bring the file to Rome to open it.

Finding her rental car out beyond the cordon, she got in and nearly screamed with excitement. Jake was alive. His baby was alive. But that also meant that

Alexandra was one of the female bodies they had pulled from the charred building. How was Jake dealing with her death?

She drove from Jake's old house outside of Tropea to Vibo Valentia, where she was set to meet at the museum parking lot outside of the castle that sat high above the city.

When Elisa rolled up and parked her rental car, she cautiously got out and stood next to her door.

Sitting across from her was an older Fiat. Stepping out was Sergio Russo, the Malavita captain from this entire province.

Glancing about, she realized the man was alone.

"You just came from Jake's house," Russo said.

"Yes."

"It's a tragedy that Jake and his family are all dead," he said.

Was this man fishing for what she knew? Maybe. But Jake knew that this man already knew that Jake and his baby had escaped. Russo had helped Jake do so. It was obvious in the video. She decided to come clean, explaining that Jake had sent her surveillance video of what had happened.

"Then you know. I will find out who did this. I gave Jake my word."

Elisa took out her phone and found the video she had downloaded. She punched in the password and let the local Mafia capo watch along with her.

"You were very brave out front," she said. "You kept them busy while Jake got his baby."

"I did what I could. But not enough. I will find these people and kill them all."

She smiled and said, "I was hoping you would say that." Elisa found the spot on the video and stopped it when it got to the right location. "This is the man."

"He was in charge?" Russo asked.

"Yes." Then she went through her phone and found a better photo, texting it directly to Russo's phone.

The Mafia man checked his phone and started to say something, but he hesitated.

"That's right. AISI officer Vito Galati."

"Your partner."

"Former partner," she corrected. "We will owe you."

Russo shook his head. "No. You will owe me nothing. I do this for Jake."

The two of them embraced like father and daughter, kissing each other on both cheeks. Then the Malavita captain got into his car and drove off.

Elisa got to her car and sat for a moment, wondering if she had done the right thing. She shrugged, smiled and started her car. Of course she had.

She drove off toward Lamezia Terme to catch a flight back to Rome.

40

Missoula, Montana

Jake had moved about Italy for a couple of days, laying low in small towns in Calabria, paying with cash. He constantly wondered if his daughter Emma missed her mother. Could children truly understand this kind of loss? Jake wasn't sure. But he knew that he understood.

Finally, he had called his billionaire benefactor, Carlos Gomez, and asked for the use of his private jet. Gomez had been surprised to hear from Jake, thinking that he had also been killed in the attack on his home by Tropea. The Spaniard had graciously offered up the jet, which had picked up Jake in Lamezia Terme, Calabria.

From there they had flown to Iceland, refueled, and continued on to Montana, getting in just a half hour ago. Gomez had a great flight crew, whom Jake had come to know personally over the past couple of years. The billionaire's people had arranged for a car to meet Jake at the small terminal, which picked him up and drove him into the south hills of the city.

By now, darkness had settled in, a nearly full moon rising above the mountains to the east. They pulled into the driveway of a nice house in an upscale neighborhood and the driver kept the engine running.

The driver of the car was a man about Jake's age. A rough looking cowboy type. He glanced back at Jake for orders.

"Could you hang tight here for a moment with the engine running?" Jake asked. "I think the baby will stay sleeping for a while."

"I'm here for you as long as needed," the driver said. "I was told to take you anywhere you want to go for as long as you need me. And don't worry about your baby. I have three kids and six grandkids. I'll keep an eye on her."

"Thanks. I appreciate that."

Jake got out and thought for a moment before closing the door. He glanced back at Emma, still asleep in her new car seat. Finally, he quietly closed the car door and let his eyes drift back to his brother's house. Kurt Jenkins had called ahead to his brother Victor and sister Jessica. They both thought Jake had been killed, and Kurt would be arriving at this time to give them details. But of course Kurt was still back in his home outside of D.C. Besides Kurt and Gomez, the only people who knew he was still alive were Elisa Murici and the Malavita capo Sergio Russo. Soon that would include his siblings.

He got to the front door and knocked lightly.

His brother Victor opened the door expecting to see the former CIA Director and instead finding his older brother. Vic was shocked, his eyes wide with disbelief.

Without saying a word, Vic hugged Jake for a long minute before pulling back. "I should have known it wasn't true," Vic said. "You're hard to kill."

"I'm tired, Vic," Jake said. He was talking not only about his present state, but with life in general.

"I imagine so. Why all the cloak and dagger?"

"That's the way I roll, Vic. That and the fact that someone obviously wants me dead." Jake hesitated before asking, "Is Jess here?"

"Yeah. She's in the media room watching football."

Jake had not seen his sister Jessica in years. He had only been back to Montana a few times in the past decade. Much of his absence was by design. With what he did for a living, family could be a liability. He didn't want to put either of them in jeopardy.

"Come on in, Jake," Vic said. "I'll get you a beer."

"In a minute. Can I stay here tonight?"

"Of course. Jess is staying in one guest room, but I have another one ready. What's the matter?"

"Nothing. I just need to tell the driver I'm good to go, and pick up a few things in the car. Could you get Jess?"

Victor looked confused. "Of course."

His brother went away and Jake peered out at the car. The driver wasn't looking back at Emma, so she must have still been sleeping.

He turned to see his little sister. Jess stopped dead in her tracks when she saw Jake. She hadn't changed much, he guessed. Her hair was a little darker auburn, and she looked like she could kick the ass of most men. Probably because she could. She worked various jobs, from river rafting guide in the summer to fishing guide, and then as a hunting wrangler in the falls. At all other times she was a true cowgirl.

Jess rushed to Jake and hugged him with considerable strength. He reciprocated, not worried about breaking her.

"Jesus, Jess," Jake said. "You're built like a lumberjack."

She pulled back and said, "Well, big brother, some of us actually work for a living. Why the hell didn't you come visit me last time you were here?"

"I think you were up in Big Sky," Jake said. "Besides, it wasn't a social visit. I was working."

"I heard you killed a guy up in Whitefish," Jess said. "What's your current number?"

Jake had never really kept track. Maybe that was a problem. Who couldn't remember how many people he had killed?

"I'm sorry," she said. "I should never ask you that."

"Alexandra is dead," Jake said. "I couldn't save her."

"We heard," Vic said. "We're so sorry. We only met her one time, but she seemed like a really special lady."

Jake gave them a half smile. "She would be disturbed that you called her a lady. She was a highly-trained operative with German Intelligence."

"You never told us that," Jess said.

Shrugging, Jake said, "Listen, I need to get a few things in the car."

"You need help?" Jess asked.

"No. Just wait here. I have something for you."

Jake went back out to the car, telling the driver he wouldn't be needed again tonight. The driver gave Jake his card, saying he would be available within a half hour for a ride anywhere Jake needed to go.

Grabbing his bags and slinging them over his shoulder, Jake unbuckled Emma's car seat and hoisted her from the back seat. He slammed the door shut and waved at the driver as he backed out.

He got to his brother's front door and hesitated.

Victor opened the door and seemed more surprised than seeing Jake alive.

"A baby?" Vic asked.

Then Jess came around and saw Emma in the car seat. "What? Oh, how adorable. Wait. This is your little baby?"

"Yeah. Meet Emma Adams. Six months old."

Jess got down on the floor next to the car seat, inspecting the new member of the family.

"This is great, Jake," Vic said. "We still haven't met your son, Karl. At least we got an early look at this one."

Jake closed the outer door behind him. Hearing Karl's name, Jake knew he needed to get in touch with him soon as well. Rumors would spread and Karl would also need to know that Jake was still with the living. He would also need to see his little sister.

"Jess, Vic, I've got a problem," Jake said.

"Just one?" Vic smiled broadly.

His brother had been married, but was now divorced. No children. His sister had never been married. And Jake had a feeling she might be a lesbian. Being in her early forties, Jake guessed Jess wouldn't be having a child anytime soon.

"I have to disappear for a while," Jake said. "And I can't do that with a young child."

Jess looked up at Jake, bewildered. Vic looked down at Emma.

Standing up quickly, Jess gave Jake a big hug again. "I'll watch her for you."

"Are you sure you can do this?" Jake asked. "You're always out in the wilderness."

"That's mostly the old me, Jake," Jess said. "I've been mostly here in Missoula giving riding lessons for the past year. I blew my knee out on an elk hunt in The Bob last fall."

Jake turned to his brother. "Could you help, Vic?"

"Of course, Jake. Not a problem."

"She's a sweet baby," Jake said. "But she needs a lot of care. You two don't exactly have experience in this area."

Jess smacked her brother in the chest. "Neither did you until six months ago."

She had a good point.

"I'll pay for everything," Jake said.

"What about Alexandra's family?" Jess asked.

"Her father is dead and her mother has dementia," Jake said. "No siblings."

"I can draw up guardianship paperwork," Vic said. "In case she needs medical care."

"Thanks," Jake said. "I will set up a wire transfer to your account. I'll make sure Alexandra's pension flows into that account."

"I'll track everything for you on a spread sheet," Vic said.

"I don't need that. I just need assurance from the both of you that Emma will be cared for properly. Like I said, this is only temporary. I just need to disappear for a while until I can find out what's going on."

They both nodded agreement.

"She can stay here," Vic said.

Jess put her hands on her hips. "I'll quit my job and take care of Emma fulltime."

Jake gave his sister another hug. Then he kissed her on the forehead. "Thanks, sis."

"Jess can move in here with me," Vic said. "God knows I have plenty of room."

Letting out a heavy sigh, Jake kneeled down and rubbed Emma's face with the back of his fingers. She was so soft. Now he guessed that Jess would have Emma on a horse as soon as she could walk. Nothing wrong with that.

Jake stood again. "I'll make sure to send my son Karl out here soon to meet his sister. Other than Karl, though, nobody is to know that I'm still alive. Do you understand?"

"Of course," Vic said.

"Sure thing," Jess added.

"All right. It's settled. I think someone offered me a beer."

Jess hurried off, saying, "Coming right up."

"How's she doing?" Jake asked Vic.

"Great. She almost got married to a younger fellow last year. But he turned out to be a cheater in dire need of a dentist."

"I heard that," Jess said, coming back with three beers and handing them to her brothers. "I only knocked out one tooth."

"And broke a couple of ribs," Vic reminded her.

Jake raised his beer and ticked it with those of his siblings. "To the Adams clan. Don't mess with us."

"You got that shit right," Jess agreed.

They all took heavy draws on their beers.

•

The next morning, Jake said goodbye to his brother and sister, and especially his little girl, Emma.

As Jake waited for the driver to pick him up, they all stood at the door.

"Where will you go?" Vic asked.

"I can't say."

"You're still packing a Glock," Jess said. "Can't go commercial with that." She held Emma like a pro on her left hip.

"I know," Jake said. "I've got a private ride."

"Nice," Jess said. "By the way, I might just keep Emma. She's a doll."

That's what he needed to hear at this very moment. Jake wasn't sure what he was doing or where he was going, but he had a feeling, like always, that his work would be dangerous. He now knew that he could never get too close to someone again. Although his relationships had produced two wonderful children, the pain that followed was nearly unbearable.

The car pulled into the driveway and Jake left his brother's house, not knowing if he would ever see any of them again. He never looked back. He just got in the back of the car and closed the door, his visage hidden behind tinted windows.

Jake sat quietly as the driver took him to the airport, where he would get on the billionaire's jet and decide where to go.

Made in the USA
Middletown, DE
28 October 2022

13679762R00201